THE LUM HAT

and other stories

Violet Jacob

THE LUM HAT
and other stories

last tales of
VIOLET JACOB

edited with an introduction
by Ronald Garden

ABERDEEN UNIVERSITY PRESS

First published 1982
Aberdeen University Press
A member of the Pergamon Group
© Ronald Garden 1982

The publisher acknowledges the
financial assistance of the
Scottish Arts Council in the
publication of this volume.

278677

British Library Cataloguing in Publication Data
Jacob, Violet
  The lum hat and other stories.
  I. Title II. Garden, Ronald
  823'.912 (F)   PR6019.A3

  ISBN 0 08 028449 3 (hard)
  ISBN 0 08 028450 7 (flexi)

PRINTED IN GREAT BRITAIN
AT THE UNIVERSITY PRESS
ABERDEEN

To the memory of

Mrs Millicent Lovett of Dun

Contents

Acknowledgements

My first debt is to the late Mrs Millicent Lovett for her cordial help to me when I was researching the work of her aunt, Violet Jacob. I am also indebted to Mrs Marjorie Lingen-Hutton, Mrs Lovett's cousin and now the owner of the copyright, for permission to publish these stories.

I have to thank Mr Michael Wright, Editor of *Country Life*, for permission to reprint "The Fifty-eight Wild Swans" and Mr Thomas Crawford, Editor of the *Scottish Literary Journal*, for "The Yellow Dog" and "Anderson". "The Wade Monument" first appeared in the *Cornhill* magazine, which ceased publication some years ago. I would also thank the Trustees of the National Library of Scotland, where Violet Jacob's typescripts of these stories are deposited, for their agreement to this publication.

Finally, I should like to record my gratitude to my friend, Dr Isobel Murray, for her great encouragement and valuable advice when I was editing the stories; and to my wife, my collaborator at all times.

R.J.B.G.

Chronology of Violet Jacob's life

1863   Violet A. M. F. Kennedy-Erskine born at House of Dun.

1870   William Henry Kennedy-Erskine of Dun, her father, died.

1891   *The Bailie MacPhee*, partly illustrated by Violet Kennedy-Erskine, published.

1894   Marriage to Major Arthur Ottway Jacob.

1895   Their only child, Arthur Henry (Harry) Jacob, born.

1897–9   Violet did many drawings of plants in India.

1899   Violet returned to Britain; her husband served in South Africa.

1902   *The Sheep-stealers* published.

1903   Publication by Violet Jacob of *The Infant Moralist*, written in collaboration with Lady Helena Carnegie, twenty-four comic poems in English, with twelve illustrations by Violet Jacob.

1904   Publication of *The Golden Heart and other Fairy Stories*. *The Interloper* published.

1905   *Verses* published.

1908   *The History of Aythan Waring* published. *Irresolute Catherine* published. At this time the Jacobs were living at Llanthornas, Hay, Herefordshire.

1909   Publication of *Stories Told by the Miller*, intended for older children.

1910   *The Fortune Hunters and Other Stories* published.

1911   Publication of *Flemington*. Beginning of long friendship with John and Susan Buchan.

1915   *Songs of Angus* published.

1916   Death of Harry Jacob.

1918   *More Songs of Angus and Others* published.

1920   The Jacobs went to live near Ludlow, Shropshire. C. M. Grieve published poems by Violet Jacob in *Northern Numbers*. At this time and for some years she was friendly with Grieve, and for many years with James Christison, Burgh Librarian of Montrose.

1921   *Bonnie Joann and Other Poems* published.

1922   *Tales of My Own Country* published.

1927   *The Northern Lights and Other Poems* published.

1928	Publication of *The Good Child's Yearbook,* with appropriate illustrations by Violet Jacob.
1931	*The Lairds of Dun* published.
1936	Violet Jacob awarded the degree of LLD by Edinburgh University. Arthur Jacob died. Violet Jacob lived at Kirriemuir, Angus, for the rest of her life.
1944	*The Scottish Poems of Violet Jacob* published.
Sept. 1946	Violet Jacob died; her grave is in Dun Churchyard.
Oct. 1977	The "short stories (Scots and English)" came to light.
May 1979	"The Yellow Dog" and "Anderson" published in *The Scottish Literary Journal.*

Introduction

It is probable that the success of Violet Jacob's poetry has overshadowed her merit as an outstanding novelist and short story writer. The result is that her prose is now out of print and difficult and expensive to obtain in antiquarian bookshops. But after the traditional period of being out of fashion, and at a time when there is a revival of interest in Scottish novelists from Hogg and Galt to Cunninghame Graham and MacDougall Hay, the appearance of a collection of largely unpublished novellas and short stories by Violet Jacob must be an interesting event in the literary world.

Violet Jacob was described by Hugh MacDiarmid in his *Contemporary Scottish Studies* in 1925 as "by far the most considerable of contemporary vernacular poets"; he had not changed his opinion fifty years later. Others who have praised her poetry since she died in 1946 include Maurice Lindsay, Albert Mackie and Douglas Young; and her poems have continued to appear in anthologies up to the present day. It has been different with her prose, and yet she was acknowledged as a prominent novelist before she had published any verses of merit.

The *Scotsman* critic wrote of her first novel, *The Sheep-Stealers*, in 1902 that it had "that rare topographical and atmospheric charm which is to be found . . . in Stevenson's *Catriona* or Hardy's *Far from the Madding Crowd*"; and the *Daily Telegraph* that her "local colour is as vivid as it is in *Lorna Doone* or *The Return of the Native*". The *Spectator* wrote that Hardy was "the writer to whom on his best . . . side Mrs Jacob is most closely related". *The Interloper*, Violet Jacob's first Angus novel, put the *Times Literary Supplement* reviewer in mind of *Jane Eyre, Cranford* and *Middlemarch*. Of *Flemington* John Buchan wrote that it was "the best Scots romance since *The Master of Ballantrae*".

Winifred Duke published in the *Northern Review* of June 1924, a long essay entitled "The Prose of Violet Jacob", in which she gave an enthusiastic and sympathetic account of the four novels, the novellas and the short stories. Hugh MacDiarmid, in his article already quoted, wrote that Violet Jacob "belongs to the small list of Scottish novelists of either sex whose work rises into the category of literature". Twenty years later, on her death in 1946, Maurice Lindsay said of Violet Jacob in his radio programme, "Chapbook" that "she first achieved notice with her novel, *The Sheep-Stealers*. It was hailed as a work of considerable promise, a promise which became performance with *The Interloper* and *Flemington*."

After this Violet Jacob's fiction received little treatment until Marion Lochhead's article, "Neglected or Forgotten", in the *Library Review* of Autumn 1976. Miss Lochhead has elsewhere written, "Both *Flemington* and *The Interloper* are surely minor classics." Then in the *Scotsman* of 25 August 1979, Alan Bold, when reviewing the May number of the *Scottish Literary Journal*, wrote, "The highlight of this issue is the appearance of two previously unpublished Scots stories by Violet Jacob. . . . I'm sure they would fascinate many general readers as well as devotees of this fine writer. It is strange that . . . they are only available to 'paid-up' members of a literary association. . . . Tom Crawford (the editor), is to be congratulated on such an editorial coup."

It is hoped that the publication of this collection of largely unpublished work will meet Mr Bold's point, and herald a new interest in Violet Jacob's prose generally.

Violet Jacob, of the family of Kennedy-Erskine of Dun, was born at the House of Dun, near Montrose, in 1863. Her most celebrated ancestor was Sir John Erskine, who was Moderator of the General Assembly of the Church of Scotland in 1565 and was a friend of both John Knox and Mary, Queen of Scots. She was also descended from King William IV by Mrs Jordan, the actress. Her early life was spent at the House of Dun, where she seems to have told stories to her brother and sister, with occasional visits abroad. In 1894 Violet Kennedy-Erskine married an Irishman, Major Arthur Jacob of the 25th Hussars, and in the following year their only child, Arthur Henry Jacob, was born. After her marriage, as well as spending two or three years in India and visiting Egypt, Violet lived in various English garrison towns to which her husband was posted, but she constantly returned to Angus. The Jacobs were also attracted to the Welsh marches; in 1908 they had a house in Herefordshire and in 1920 in Shropshire. This may show the influence of Violet's Welsh mother. The marriage of Violet and Arthur Jacob was clearly a happy one, but a great grief was that Harry Jacob, as he was called, died of wounds in France in 1916. Arthur Jacob died in 1936. Thereafter Violet Jacob herself went to live in Kirriemuir, where she died in 1946.

Apart from some short stories, Violet Jacob's prose work is entirely set in either Angus or the Anglo-Welsh borderland. Even before her son's death there is a sense of tragedy in her novels. Only a few of her England-based short stories are less serious, and in none of her work is there a feeling of anything lush or cosy.

Nevertheless, Violet Jacob's first published work, written in collaboration with W. D. Campbell, was a comic narrative poem in Scots, *The Bailie MacPhee*. But though she was evidently interested in the Scots language from an early age her first prose, published in 1902, was a novel, *The Sheep-Stealers*, set among the hills and valleys of Hereford and Brecon. The period was the eighteen-forties and the hero, Rhys Walters, a dare-devil Welsh farmer, became the leader of a band of rioters.

These men were protesting against what they considered the unjust and excessive tolls which had lately been put on the turnpike roads. They were disguised in women's clothes and their leader was known as "Rebecca". During an attack on a toll-house, the gate-keeper, the father of Walters's discarded mistress was killed, and Walters was blamed for the murder, though another "Rebecca" rioter had struck the fatal blow. Walters was pursued by an officer of the local Yeomanry, the squire's son, but succeeded in going into hiding at the cottage of George Williams. Williams had been blackmailed into stealing sheep for an Abergavenny butcher, and on one occasion Walters had helped Williams to steal a sheep. Emerging from his hideout from time to time, Walters had some love passages with Isoline, the rather shallow and cool rose-and-white beauty who was engaged to the squire's son, and who did not realise that Walters was "Rebecca". However, on the squire's son's coming into money, she deserted Walters and eloped with him. When Walters heard of the marriage he was filled with despair and threw himself over a precipice to his death. Rhys Walters, despite his reckless and selfish character, is not an anti-hero and his ending is felt as tragic.

It is interesting to note Violet Jacob's relative sexual frankness in a novel published more than three-quarters of a century ago, as when she wrote that Rhys Walters's mother could not comprehend that "the husband should remain the lover, the wife the mistress".

After the publication of a volume of comic poems in English and another of fairy stories, Violet Jacob published in 1904 her first novel set in Angus, *The Interloper*, again in the earlier part of the nineteenth century.

Gilbert Speid, the interloper, was acknowledged by the laird of Whanland as his son and heir. In reality he was the illegitimate son of Robert Fullarton, another still-living Angus laird, by the elder Speid's long-dead wife. Gilbert Speid, a stalwart young man, with a rather heavy face, returned from Spain to become the new laird of Whanland. He soon encountered a remarkable character, Lady Eliza Lamont, noted for her horsemanship and her red wig. She had never married, having failed to win Fullarton's love. As Gilbert Speid's mother had been her successful rival, Lady Eliza disliked him, and all the more when Speid and her ward, the slender, quiet Cecilia Raeburn, fell in love. But Speid, on discovering his illegitimacy, felt himself unworthy of the girl and went back to Spain. Meanwhile Cecilia, to please her benefactress, agreed to marry a second suitor, Fordyce, unless Speid came back within a year. Through the intervention of another elderly woman, a fishwife with whom both the lovers had made friends, a letter was sent to Spain to encourage Speid to return to Scotland. This he did and arrived just in time to marry Cecilia himself.

The Interloper gives a good picture of Scottish society of the early nineteenth century, and Scots words and idioms are much used in the dialogue, but the *Spectator* critic wrote that "Mrs Jacob is no devotee of the kailyard cult, following in regard to the use of dialect, the excellent example set by Sir Walter".

In the following year the first collection of Violet Jacob's poems, *Verses*, appeared. In 1908 she published two works of fiction: *The History of Aythan Waring*, a full-length novel, and *Irresolute Catherine*, a novella of 25,000 words. The scene of both books is again the Anglo-Welsh borderland in the first half of the nineteenth century.

Aythan and Eustace Waring were cousins and wards of Matthew Bridges, the squire of Crishowell, who had loved Aythan's mother and intended her son to be his heir. However, when nearly sixty he married a rather hard young woman, Hester Corbett. But six years later Bridges' horse threw him and he was killed. Hester was now at Crishowell with two men, both younger than herself: Aythan, whom she disliked, and the handsome Eustace, to whom she was soon secretly engaged. Aythan left Crishowell and soon fell in love with Barbara Troup, a lively young horsewoman.

Some local men had been making beer illicitly, and a spy of the Excise was attacked by them in the Roodchurch where the malting was going on.

Aythan was accused of the attempted murder, tried, found guilty and condemned to death. But an epidemic of typhus struck the village, and one of the victims, troubled in conscience, confessed that he had seen Aythan leave the Roodchurch before the spy was struck down. As a result Aythan was granted a free pardon. The novel ends with Eustace and Hester dying of typhus, and Aythan and Barbara happily married. In summary, a real melodrama, though the style is sober.

Irresolute Catherine is a slighter production altogether, though it too holds the reader's interest. In this novella, as in the two Anglo-Welsh novels, Violet Jacob's quiet, and sometimes grim, painting of the background of the countryside, the lanes, the valleys and the hillsides is highly effective and this may have caused contemporary reviewers to write of her as having some of the atmospheric charm of Hardy.

Violet Jacob's travels are reflected in her next book—*The Fortune Hunters and other Stories*—which was issued in 1910. The title story is a novella of 19,000 words, of which the heroine is Rosamund Slade, a wealthy but orphaned young woman, and her various suitors. Most of the stories had previously appeared in magazines and on the whole they do not reach the literary standards of the novels.

In 1911 *Flemington*, Violet Jacob's second Angus and last full-length novel, was published.

Archie Flemington was the son of a Jacobite who had died at the exiled court of James II. He was brought up by his handsome but formidable grandmother; she had become a Whig because of her ill-treatment at the Jacobite court and had influenced Archie to become a British government agent or spy.

The tall, twenty-six year old Flemington contrived an introduction to James Logie, a Jacobite agent some ten years older than himself, at the house, near Montrose, of Lord Balnillo, Logie's brother. Flemington and Logie came to like each other.

It was 1745 and a British naval barque, the *Venture*, was captured by the Jacobites at Montrose. On a nearby island Archie Flemington and Logie became engaged in hand to hand combat, after which Archie was left stunned. Logie joined Prince Charles's southward-marching army, but when the Jacobites were forced to retreat Flemington joined the Hanoverian troops as intelligence officer to the Duke of Cumberland. Logie escaped unhurt at Culloden; Flemington was slightly wounded there but ordered, in company with a Captain Callandar, to capture his old friend and enemy, James Logie. Flemington could not bring himself to do so; he sent a warning to Logie and himself surrendered to

Callandar. Madam Flemington's plea to Cumberland for mercy for her grandson was brusquely refused and he was shot by a firing squad. In the last chapter after the rebellion was over Callandar handed to Logie in Holland a letter from Flemington, an "apologia pro vita sua".

This unusual and powerful story, written from the unpopular angle, is probably Violet Jacob's most memorable novel.

Between 1911 and 1921 Violet Jacob published three volumes of poems, mainly in Scots. She had also been writing short stories with an Angus background and they were published in 1922 as *Tales of My Own Country*. Most of these eleven stories are approximately of her own time; one of them, "Annie Cargill", is a grim story of the supernatural.

Many of the most notable characters are women: "Auntie" Thompson, an elderly villager who admirably coped with her nephew's snobbish fiancée; the persecuted servant-lass who went off with a gipsy; Euphemia, the redoubtable farm-worker; the ferryman's daughter, whose miser father, "Thievie", drowned with his gold; and the Montrose shopgirl, who lost her sweetheart, Falconer, in a contest with a ship's figure-head. The themes are universal, yet the countryside, the sea and characters are essentially Scottish.

Tales of My Own Country are, on the whole, more deeply felt than *The Fortune Hunters and Other Stories*, the characters are more true to life and the backgrounds more authentic. There is also the splendid Scots dialogue.

Violet Jacob continued to write short stories and poems from time to time. A story with an English background, "The Wade Monument" appeared in the *Cornhill Magazine* in February 1921, and a Scots story, "The Fifty-eight Wild Swans", in *Country Life* of August 1926.

In 1944, when the poet was eighty-one, *The Scottish Poems of Violet Jacob* was published by Oliver and Boyd. On 20 June 1944, shortly after the publication of this last book of verse, Violet Jacob offered her publishers "a book of short stories (Scots and English). The two principal and longest of these", she wrote, "have not yet appeared in print". I found this letter in the archives of Oliver and Boyd in the National Library of Scotland, and also their answer that they could not publish the stories at that time because of wartime paper rationing, though they hoped to do so later.

But in September, 1946, Violet Jacob died at Marywell House, Kirrie-muir. She had named her niece, Mrs Millicent Lovett, as her executrix. This was a period of travail for Mrs Lovett, for about this time both her husband and her mother died; and because she was living in Shropshire, she asked an Angus friend to help her to deal with Violet Jacob's effects.

Mrs Lovett did not return to Montrose until some eight years ago when she became the twenty-first Laird of Dun. She was the source of most of my knowledge about Violet Jacob's life. In 1976, in conversation with me, Mrs Lovett said that to her knowledge no manuscripts of her aunt's existed. Late in 1977, however, she wrote to me that her Angus friend had handed her a portfolio of Violet Jacob manuscripts which she had been looking after for Mrs Lovett for thirty years. This portfolio, besides a few poems and magazine articles, contained the lost stories. After I had examined them, these manuscripts were deposited in the National Library of Scotland. Mrs Lovett died in June 1980.

There are three short stories with a Scottish background: "The Fifty-eight Wild Swans", already mentioned as published in *Country Life*; and "The Yellow Dog" and "Anderson", published in the May 1979 number of the *Scottish Literary Journal.* There are four other short stories: "The Wade Monument", also mentioned above as published but uncollected; "Business and Pleasure", "Secret Intelligence" and "Madame Chardinet". In addition, and probably more important, there are two novellas: "The Lum Hat" and "Banny Firelocks".

Both "The Fifty-eight Wild Swans" and "Anderson" contain a portrait of a small boy. The chief character in "The Fifty-eight Wild Swans", Jimmy Strachan, is, however, a rather "thrawn" old man, though not so extreme in his obstinacy as "Thievie". "The Yellow Dog" resembles "Annie Cargill" in having a supernatural element, but is notable in being written almost entirely in a rich Scots.

"The Wade Monument" is like "Annie Cargill" in that Alured Wade too was wronged and was commemorated in a laconic tombstone, and like "Annie Cargill", and "Behind the Wall" in *The Fortune Hunters,* it contains a ghostly female visitant.

"Madame Chardinet" is the only story that Violet Jacob ever set in France, a country she had several times visited, and nowhere else in her fiction does she give such a striking picture of a vindictive old woman. "Secret Intelligence" is the story of a sustained deception, while "Business and Pleasure" is a kind of love story with a surprise ending.

Violet Jacob was clearly working on the two novellas when she died. "Banny Firelocks" is of 64 typewritten pages, but two and a half pages are missing; the whole would have amounted to 15,000 words. "The Lum Hat" is 90 typewritten pages long, but five pages are missing; including these, it would have amounted to 23,000 words. It has been possible in each case to supply reasonable connections; the author left a few relevant handwritten notes. Some minor obscurities in the text, which Violet Jacob might have clarified in a final revision, have been left unaltered.

"Banny Firelocks" resembles the earlier novella, *Irresolute Catherine*, in being set in the Anglo-Welsh borderland in the middle of the nineteenth century and having as its heroine a girl with two lovers; but there the resemblance ends. Barbara Langland's nickname of "Firelocks" came from her flowing copper-coloured hair, appropriate to one of her lively personality. She is one of Violet Jacob's most attractive characters.

"The Lum Hat" is only two thousand words shorter than *Irresolute Catherine*, which was published as an independent volume; and it is possible that at one time Violet Jacob may have contemplated the publication of "The Lum Hat" separately from her other stories, as in the letter already referred to from Oliver and Boyd, they reminded her that it was at their office.

The opening scene of "The Lum Hat" is an east coast seaport, clearly Montrose and certainly resembling that town as depicted in *Flemington*. The heroine, Christina Mill, though a more complicated personality than Rosamund in *The Fortune Hunters*, seems rather too delicate and ladylike; Andrew Baird, captain of the barque *Sirius*, whom she marries, is a selfish and insensitive young man like Eustace in *Aythan Waring*. But it is a dramatic tale unique in Violet Jacob's fiction for containing an account of a storm, which the author herself had probably experienced several times, and for the brief description of the sexual relationship between Christina and her husband.

In these short stories and novellas Violet Jacob showed that she had not lost, with increasing years, her sense of humour or her ability to tell a story and to convey character, but that her powers as a writer—and a writer of spare, understated vigorous prose—had remained with her until the end of her life.

◄• The Lum Hat •►

I

Christina Mill is so hard a person to portray, both physically and mentally, that there is no help but to describe the small photograph—taken in the very early days of the art—which is the only record of her looks. She was almost twenty-seven when it was done though she looks much younger. It is set in an absurd little leather case with a clasp. She is not beautiful, scarcely even good-looking; she wears a turnover collar like a schoolboy's, but soft and scallop-edged, and a dark velvet spencer. Short, hanging curls cover her ears, no ringlets, but the solid sausage sort; her parted hair lies smooth till it joins them. Her face is a longish oval and her lips, more heavy than thin, are a little parted.

This is a mere inventory of clothes and feature. Expression is what matters and here the difficulty begins. It is self-contained and innocent, reserved, yet immature. The smooth, stolid face seems scarcely grown-up and the grace of velvet and silk belies it. Her shapely long fingers with their rings and her braceleted wrists might belong to the placid hands of a far older woman. They look so settled.

The house she lived in, in the east coast Scottish seaport still stands, a trifle back from the street, in the Bow Butts, just where it joins Ferry Street on the way to the quays. In her day, if you walked fifty yards down Ferry Street you could see the windjammers lying alongside with the glittering water beyond them. It is a plain three-storied house with tall narrow windows. The flagged enclosure along its frontage is so much straitened by the low wall dividing it from the street that it has an air of being on tip-toe in order to get above its adjuncts and to be demanding, in the name of gentility, to be allowed more space. A couple of slim-stemmed ornamental trees are close to the windows.

Four people lived in it: Christina, her father, a maid-servant and Ann Wishart, the cook; for William Mill, who was manager of the local Bank of Angus, had some means and his daughter had no need to spoil her

1

refined hands with housework. She kept them for the naive bits of fancy work that slaked the artistic thirst of her contemporaries. Sometimes she would pretend to help the cook when preserving was going on, but Ann, who had been of the household years before Christina grew up, discouraged this, because of her passionate belief that the gentry should keep the pose thrust upon them by God.

The banker's wife was a pale myth to her child. The recollection of ourselves at four years old are only flashes of unoutlined scenes. She remembered the figure of someone sitting by a downstairs window with a red curtain—still in its place—behind her and a thin face on the pillow of the four-poster to which her father still repaired nightly, and that was all. The solid female presence which had once been her aunt Isabella Mill and was now her aunt Isabella Halket had obliterated the other one. Isabella Mill had come to the rescue of her bereaved brother, a stout resourceful woman with whom Ann Wishart had never contrived to quarrel openly, probably because of the indolence which inclined the lady to leave the major troubles of housekeeping to somebody else; she would have liked to be upside with Ann but her robust, everday perceptions told her that Ann was best left alone. For all her assured demeanour, caution lurked in her. Christina, whose attitude from childhood had been a contemplative one, would look at her aunt with the half-smile that sat so often on her parted lips. She watched everything, seeing nothing but the outside and contented with that. Yet there was something faintly curious in her mind, a semi-conscious fingering at the doorkey of life. But nothing that disturbed her.

Many people, though they may be happy, never let themselves formulate the idea. Christina had been saved from that misfortune by reason of her conception of what happiness was; she mistook contentment for it. She would put down her fancy work complacently, thinking of her advantages, of her good clothes, of her father's uniform kindness—nothing positive or emotional, but something to be counted on. Then there was the consideration of friends and neighbours, and even of those who were neither; who lived in mean streets and smaller houses and who knew her only by seeing her on the pavements, a figure set apart, creditable and established. It would have astonished her very much had she known that, to a large part of the town, she was Miss "Lummie" Mill and she would not have liked it. She shared the homely word with her father whose unusually tall "chimney-pot" hat had caused him to be known as "Lummie Mill" to a population devoted (as all Scottish towns are) to nicknames. That hat was as much a part of the community as the wooden Highlander who had stood for some generations at a tobacconist's door in the Seagate, or the spire of the parish kirk. Lummie was a thin man with a nervous jocular manner much mimicked by his clerks. People continually said they were surprised at the success in life of such a fool, forgetting that, though he was no genius, he had two valuable qualities, a dislike of giving offence and a habit of leaving things he did not understand to those who did.

The family sat in the first pew under the gallery in the parish church where they could be clearly observed by their fellow worshippers; Christina passive and aloof in her silks and velvet spencer, her father with pursed lips, bald and attentive to his bible, with the lum hat, like a third presence, occupying the end of the long red cushion. Girls would look with awe on Christina's dress, loitering about the church door to get a nearer view of it when the kirk "came out". She was aware of this and it pleased a vanity not personal enough to be offensive. It was not herself that she was so satisfied with but her circumstances and had it been her own beauty that impressed the girls she would have found it less interesting. She thought little about beauty; she did not possess it and it had never occurred to her to desire it.

It was only of late years that father and daughter had sat alone with the lum hat. Christina was twenty when her aunt was courted by a well-to-do insurance agent who transported her to Gayfield Square, Edinburgh. Uncle Halket, as Christina called him, came little into her life and died suddenly five years after his marriage. The widow moved into a smaller house for she was not left as well off as she had expected to be and her visits to her brother grew longer. She would have liked to come back to her old place permanently but Christina showed no desire to give up the reins to which she had grown accustomed and Ann Wishart was determined she should not do so; Mrs Halket knew that as well as if she had been told it.

The reason for her disappointing circumstances as the relict of a comparatively rich man was that much, including the Gayfield Square house, had been left to Aeneas, his son by his first wife. He had no ill-will at Isabella but he had liked her predecessor better and he was extremely fond of his son; for Aeneas had an excellent position with a firm of glove manufacturers in France, and while little more than a boy had shown such industry and capabilities that his father had been given to understand his future to be assured, should he go on as he had begun. He was sent to the Edinburgh branch of the business though his duties often took him abroad.

3

Christina had never had a lover nor a ghost of a love affair—the only sign of a man's interest in her had come from Aeneas Halket. They had met at her aunt's house on one of her visits there and the young man, whose profession had made him notice woman's hands, had told his stepmother that he had never seen more beautiful ones than those of her niece. Once, he had said to Christina that a cast ought to be taken of them and she had blushed; but the idea seemed to her so odd that she had taken little pleasure in it. But she looked at them carefully in her room that night when she was undressing and wondered if they were really so beautiful. Faces were beautiful, she knew, but she had never thought about hands.

Not long after this Aeneas spent a fortnight in France and brought her back a little coloured picture of St Cecilia sitting at a musical instrument with her long tapered fingers touching the keys. It was very pretty and French and affected with lilies in the background and she kept it on her bedroom mantelpiece. Sometimes she thought of Aeneas and wondered how much he liked her. She had no girl friends with whom to discuss the point; for they were all mere acquaintances, but Ann Wishart, whose long service had made her one of the family, discovered from whom the picture had come and commented on it.

"A'm thinkin' the young gentleman should hae kent better nor send a Popish thing the like o' yon till a young leddy," she remarked.

"But it was very kind of him," replied Christina.

"It was an attention, surely."

"Oh, do you think so, Ann?"

Ann was an avowed expert of custom and deportment. The girl waited, open-eyed, for a reply. Getting none, she repeated her words.

"Heuch!—they Halkets!" exclaimed Ann, enigmatically.

Perhaps Ann was the only one of the household who looked beyond the daily round; Lummie Mill glided along on a path of ledgers from one year's end to another, satisfied to return to a long evening and the snug company of some casually dropping-in neighbour. He liked Christina to preside at the eight o'clock tea tray, silent and well-attired. The neighbour, from civility, would address her now and again with that mixture of sprightly yet deferential patronage which people often use to the children of rich men, though she had, as the French say, "coifféd Sainte Caterine" and her flounces went ill with his attempt to adjust himself.

Aeneas was not inclined to forget Christina. She occupied his thoughts often. He did not know what it was that attracted him besides her hands. She had little to say and the half-smile she seemed to use to supplement her want of words would have irritated some people. He admitted that, but he was not irritated, He was dark himself, and her shining pale hair pleased his eye. He liked her effortlessness to please by any of the accepted charms of girlhood. It struck him as an original thing, for he had not learnt yet exactly how to estimate the obvious.

[The rest of Aeneas's thought's about Christina at this stage are lost.]

II

Martinmas Fair came. It had no interest for Christina but Ann liked it and persuaded her to go.

"It may be a little coarse," said Ann, "but we winna bide lang and ye haena been out these three-fower days."

So they started. The Fair was in full swing and they were engulfed. Whistles blew, men roared, women roared too; children ran between grown-up people's legs, dodging the cuffs of their elders. Penny trumpets brayed in falsetto.

Christina stood and looked round on the crowd. Many were drunk and more were on the way to it. A dog-fight had started and a knot of women, under whose feet the savage din had arisen as suddenly as a gale of wind, flew asunder screaming. The girl had little mind for the rough business of returning by the way she came. Ann had some domestic errand on hand so she left her and turned down a quiet street leading to the links.

There was no golf course in those days. Along the grassy spaces she would walk home away from the pandemonium of the town. She strolled along between town and sea. On her right hand the tall, beautiful steeple of the parish kirk held its flying buttresses against the sky and over the roofs crowded below it. The sun was near the horizon and the smoke from many chimneys, the varied skyline with its slopes and steepnesses and angles, caught the smouldering sundown and became welded into one vision of romance like the embodiment of the soul of a town. Christina saw nothing of these things.

On her left the sea lay cold and hidden by the dunes along the shore. Its voice, like the voice of a shell held to the ear, had the breath of a far away history reaching from childhood to death, from time to the end of time. The white finger of the lighthouse stood up where the river, having passed the shipping, ran out to the bar.

Not far from her was moored one of those vehicles that everybody except those who own them call "caravans". A woman sat on the step.

What interested Christina was the basket hanging above her head full of small red and green feather brooms. She had seen some like them in the High Street but the crowd had prevented her from getting near to buy one. She stopped, hesitating, and would have pulled out her purse had she been sure of the propriety of speaking to a person between whom and herself was so great a gulf. It was no vulgar pride which impeded her but a distrust of the unknown and the shadow of Ann Wishart.

The woman, as a citizen of the world, had the advantage of her and stepping down, came forward.

"What is't ye're seekin?" she enquired.

She seemed a few years older than Christina and she had all the weight of a human being whose position—whatever it may be—is so well defined that there is no need to insist upon it. There was nothing of the apology of the vagrant in her voice and the girl saw that the waggon was freshly painted; the horse—though Christina did not notice this—was well rugged up with a piece of sacking. The woman was unlike anyone she had ever spoken to before; she was definitely good-looking with hair of the corn-coloured yellow never seen but on the heads of the hatless; it was dressed with a resolute neatness that in itself amounted to beauty. It looked as if a hairdresser had done it and as if nobody, not a hairdresser, could ever undo it again. Her eyes were light hazel and she was wrapped in a green plaid.

"I want a little broom," said Christina. "Like those," she added, pointing to the basket.

"Come awa' an' ye'll get ane," said the other.

Christina followed her with a fluttering sense of risk. She did not know whether she would be sorry or glad just now to see Ann Wishart. Sorry, she thought, perhaps.

The woman unhooked the basket and took out a brush of each colour; the western light made a crimson blur and a green one as she held them up.

"The reid's bonnie," she said, gravely. Though she was friendly she seemed as little likely to smile as an animal.

Christina bought and paid for the red one.

"I saw a man in the fair with some like that," she said.

"Aye. Yon's ma man. He's there."

"Do you always come to it?" asked the girl, prolonging her adventuresomeness now that it seemed so harmless.

6

"Na. We hae na been this road afore. We gang doon aboot Pairth and Edinburgh."

"That's a long way," observed Christina with a little sententious air.

The other smiled for the first time.

"It's nae sae far as England."

"But do you ever go there?"

"Aye, div we."

"To England in that cart?"

"And what for no? Maybe ye've never seen London."

Christina shook her head.

"Aweel, we gang nae far oot-by it."

"And have you been in it and seen the streets?"

"Aye, have I. We got a lad tae mind the horse and we ga'ed in and got a sight o't, ma man and me."

Christina's amazed face stirred something in her companion's vanity and loosened her tongue.

"Ye'll see a' thing in London," she went on. "Sic-like shops ye wadna believe't and muckle hooses for the gentry. And them that rides i' their twa-horse machines has twa men tae drive them—ane sitting up aside the ither. And gin ye stand still ye'll see mair grand folk ganging past ye in a meenit than ye'd see here in a towmont. Ye should gang an' tak a sicht o't yersel!"

"Oh, but I could not do that," said Christina.

"And what for no? You that has plenty siller."

"My father never leaves here. We are always here."

"Weel," rejoined the woman, reflectively. "I couldna thole tae bide in ae place yon gait. I dinna ken what I wad dae. But ye'll weary, na doubt. Fegs, I shouldna like tae be you though I'll no say but ye hae a bonnie goon on ye and ye'll likely be gettin' meat till yer denner ilka day."

Christina was silent. It was difficult to know what to say to such a strange person: nor was she accustomed to be pitied, certainly not by a woman who sold brooms by the wayside.

She was turning away.

"Ye should get a man," said the other. "Get you a man that'll tak' ye awa and gie ye a sicht of the world."

Christina had almost opened her mouth to reply that there was no man she knew who was likely to do that, but some inherent feminine instinct stopped her. She bade her acquaintance good evening, a little ruffled, and went homewards.

As she went, she thought of Aeneas Halket and wished again that she

7

knew his real feelings for her. She had read about love in the decorous books of her day and reading, had stood aloof looking on at the story from the detached standpoint of one watching the life of a street through the cold window pane. She supposed, from what she read, that gentlemen made their proposals on one knee, expressing themselves well as they did so and she gathered from Ann's criticisms of such things that sometimes they wrote letters expressing themselves even better. She considered the paraphernalia of weddings, the satin and flowers and excitement, delightful. One day they might be her lot and she knew there was generally "a wedding journey". That would be the time for seeing the world and that was what the woman had meant in her case. She decided to tell no one about her. Ann would not approve of her stopping to talk to strangers of that kind.

III

The woman with the brooms had began to fade a little from Christina's mind. There was rather more stir in the seafaring world that winter and this had its effect upon the town and even upon the household of Lummie Mill; for a four-masted barque came in in December to load timber for Adelaide and the carpenters were soon busy in her; for now, at the end of a long cruise she was to be refitted to sail in the spring.

It so happened that the captain of the *Sirius* was related to the manager of another branch of the Bank of Angus and he carried a letter of introduction to Lummie from his colleague. He was described in it as one of the best captains in his line and one considered by his owners as a rising sun. "You will find Andrew Baird good company," said the writer. "He has seen a deal of the world and should be something of a variety to you and Miss."

But the captain had little need of his cousin's good offices. He had soon found himself a suitable lodging and a footing among the principal people of the town. He had no family to claim his attention on shore and he was anxious to be near his ship while the workmen were in her. His owners, willing to do things handsomely for one of their best seamen, had given him what was almost a free hand in some improvements he had asked for in his cabin accommodation and he meant to avail himself of this to the full. He was a young man to have a ship like the *Sirius*, which was reckoned the pick of her line. He was aware of that and was sensible that behoved him to make others aware of it too.

On the second Sunday after the *Sirius* came in he was to be seen in the parish kirk having determined to run his eye over the townspeople before becoming acquainted with any of them. He took the seat shown him and having disposed of his hat, he watched the entrance of the congregation, his arms folded across his broad chest. He was dressed well and with care and he thought that, though he had spent most of his thirty-six years in ships, he looked just the same as his neighbours. In this he made a vast mistake for he was as much like the town-bred men about him as a bull terrier is like a spaniel. But he had not a rough appearance and on this Sunday morning he was rather sleek though his dark clipped beard was coarse and his face tanned.

In a small town a stranger in church is a godsend. People surveyed Baird openly over their bibles and covertly between their fingers and those fortunate enough to be able to see him without moving anything but their eyes behaved with a plainness that did not become them. Straight opposite, under the gallery, Christina and her father were compelled to see him whether they wished it or not and he was compelled to see them. As something unusual, arresting, he riveted Christina and gave her an indefinite feeling that he ought not to be there; his unusualness seemed to disturb the decorum of a church. He did not exactly attract her although she took her customary passive pleasure in anything she had not seen before; and when her father hurried out at the end of the service, whispering to her that this was evidently the captain of the big ship and that he must introduce himself to him without delay, dumbness of both tongue and spirit came over her.

As they waited outside on the kirk pavement—that meeting place of all and sundry—with the tall steeple above it, she stood back alone. To avoid setting her eyes on Baird as he came through the church door, she looked upwards at the great mass of stonework towering pointed above them to its weather vane and received from the moving clouds beyond it the sensation of being under something that was falling on her. Turning abruptly to earth, she met a direct look from Captain Baird who was replacing his hat.

It was not from "Lummie" Mill that his daughter got her placidity. In some things the banker was very active. Minor hospitalities, inquiries after health and trivial exchanges of civility were dear to him. Baird, who had not known of his kinsman's letter, was astonished at being accosted and shewed it; but he was not displeased, for Christina's shining hair and detached look gave his generally robust fancy a new and curious pleasure. She represented an unknown craft on his horizon.

9

"A fine, easy fellow—a very pleasant way with him," said Lummie after they parted. "He mustn't think himself altogether a stranger after all Dixon wrote to me about him. "You'll have to look out your best fal-lals when he comes to drink tea."

"His beard is very black," said the girl, accustomed to the incurved, silky whiskers of her contemporaries.

"He's a sailor, you see, my dear," replied Lummie, who was a loose reasoner.

"And does that make them black?"

She spoke without a touch of sarcasm.

"No, no, nonsense—I mean sailors are different."

It was strange that Baird made her think of the woman with the brooms; both were things whose purpose seemed obscure—almost like forbidden things. She was faintly uncomfortable in their presence. They touched some sleeping thing in her mind which feared to be awakened. Perhaps, after all there was some imagination in her, inherited from some sources beyond her memory, buried below the mountain of small satisfactions that made up her easy life. She had only exchanged a few unmeaning words with Baird and he had appeared to be much more aware of her father's talk than of herself; yet, in spite of her uncomfortableness, she was glad he was coming to the house. She told Ann of the meeting.

There had been a great deal of exaggerated talk in the town about the *Sirius*. It was said the Baird was part owner of her and that his cabin was to have silver fittings; that this was to be his last voyage and that he was going to retire, some way on the right side of forty, to an opulent leisure when it was over; but Baird's age was the only point that was right. Ann had heard it, with even more exaggeration and she announced that he meant to settle in the place and live in great style in one of the new turreted houses with Venetian blinds that were springing up the landward side. But though she was impressed she would not have been herself if she had not asserted some superiority, even over such a dazzling person.

"You'd wonder that Mr Mill would ask the like o' they sailor-folk intill his hoose," she said.

"But he is Mr Dixon's cousin," replied Christina, with the least hint of reproof in her voice.

Ann made no answer. She saw the force of this, but she and her household had got to be superior to something. She turned away to her oven.

It was scarcely a week later that the skipper, having dined at the house in the Bow Butts, followed his host up to the drawing-room. Late dinner was then a rare enough institution to confer a breath of distinction on those who consumed it, but the after-dinner tea table lingered, though coffee was never thought of. Baird could be both genial and morose. Mill had not diverted him much, yet he felt that he was at least surrounded by a refinement not to be matched at sea. Isabella Halket had, on her visits, grafted into the household some of the ornamental details of life to which she had grown accustomed in Edinburgh and her niece had accepted them with her usual unquestioning docility.

The girl sat very silent during their meal. She was feeling the guest to be less of a responsibility than she had expected and she sat serene in her voluminous silk dress, a little too rich for her years; her hair shone and she looked up with her dimly expectant half-smile as the two men came in. She made such a picture of feminine suitability as she paused in her tatting that Baird, responsive to the good wine he had drunk, took in the spectacle of the room of which she was the culminating point, with facile pleasure.

He did not sit down by her with the directness of social assurance but stood on the hearth with Lummie before nerving himself to do so. He would accomplish it in the end; whilst any action that suited him seemed simple enough on deck he felt it to be rather different in a house, though he concealed the fact very well. The atmosphere of this place attracted him. He liked its suggestion of solid worldly advantage, though he could hardly have found anything further from the world than this decorous, monotonous drawing room. As he took his teacup from Christina's hand he drew a chair nearer to her table. She might have linked him to it by some commonplace remark but she said nothing. He did not know how to speak to a girl like the one before him, she was so utterly different from the women he had come across; but he was not really embarrassed because he had not the habit of being so and he knew that she was just a chit whose circumstances were all that was to blame for her divergence from type.

"I wish I could get as good a cup of tea as this on board," he said.

"I hear your ship is to have a very fine cabin," she observed, timidly.

"I'll see to *that*," he laughed. "We poor fellows have a right to some comforts and I mean to have the best accommodation in the line. She's the biggest ship they've got—but I suppose a young lady has little interest in a ship."

"It is a schooner, I suppose?" asked Christina, who had heard the word and supposed all seagoing vessels to be alike except in size. He laughed a little louder.

11

"No, no, she's a barque—a four-masted barque. I doubt you don't go often to the harbour, Miss Mill".

"I never go there." She was quite complacent, though she had coloured.

"Well, when they've finished her you should step down with Mr Mill and look at her. There will be something to show you then."

She turned, pleased, to her father.

"Yes, indeed we will come," said Lummie, "I've never been on anything bigger than the ferry. But you'll not need to sail off with us, Captain. They would never do without me here, you know," he added, with his high-pitched laugh which always doubled him up a little.

"I won't do that. At any rate I'll put *your father* ashore," rejoined Baird, looking hard at Christina.

"I should be very much frightened on a ship," she said.

"And why, Miss?"

"There might be a storm."

"And, if there were, you'd be as safe as you are ashore."

"Oh—surely not—"

"And why, surely not? You might get a slate off a roof on your head, or be blown against the wall of a house."

"Very true, very true, indeed," said Lummie with the sudden gravity of one who bows to resistless logic.

"And of course I know there is the lifeboat," said Christina, willing to show that she understood at least something of what was being talked about.

Baird checked the smile on his lips.

"You'd never need that."

She was silent, a little reassured. He had been many voyages, round the world, perhaps, and had great experience.

"And where will you go, when you sail away from here?"

"Adelaide, next voyage. A fine place, too."

"It is the capital of South Australia, is it not? Just as Edinburgh is the capital of Scotland?"

He nodded.

"A fine city, Miss Mill. Everything a man can want when he comes off the sea. Good company—the best."

He cast a sophisticated glance at his host and got the acquiescent laugh from him that he would have got for any statement not definitely funereal.

"Fine shops, fine streets, fine houses, fine living. I remember being at a great banquet there. The owners of another line were entertaining their own skippers and ours. Their ladies were there too, fine women, some of them and they knew how to show themselves off. There was one of them a real beauty. We dined off silver plate—everything of the best."

"Is it a very gay place then?" asked Christina.

"We thought so, all the time we were there. It may be a lonely life at sea, Miss Mill, but you can make up for that in these foreign places."

"Yes, no doubt," exclaimed Mill with his mild knowingness, "if you are captain of a big ship like the *Serious*. Why did they call her the *Serious*, by the way?"

"*Sirius*, Sir—the dog-star."

"To be sure, to be sure."

Baird did not know what to make of his host. In general, men looked on Mill as a fool. The skipper only knew him in one aspect and his social judgements were of a rough order. He was feeling an amused contempt for Mill which did not extend itself to his daughter. She was even more simple, he considered; but simplicity, which sat ill on a bank manager sat well enough on a girl. It would soon pass, given the right experiences, and he rather admired a sheltered delicacy, in theory. He had enjoyed his dinner, for Ann Wishart, though she might affect to look down on seafarers, was ready to pamper the whole race sooner than abate a farthing's worth of credit from her particular household.

Christina woke up a little that evening. The guest was ready to talk about his voyages and though the seamanship that set him so high in his profession conveyed absolutely nothing to his hearers, his accounts of that rich merchant life existing in the great seaports of the world fascinated the banker and was also fascinating Christina. He made a sequel—a grand sequel to the humble volume opened for her by the woman on the links. She was almost bewildered when, Baird having gone and her father's cackling laugh ceased with the shutting of the house door, she had heard the chain being put up.

She dawdled over her undressing and stood some time in front of Saint Cecilia simpering among her lilies. But she did not so much as give a thought to her.

Winter wore slowly into Spring and the town went through its changes of aspect. Grey "haar" sweeping in from the sea, obliterating it so that, inland, there seemed nothing to tell of its presence but the voice of the steeple clock. Cold sunlight at times laid a hand on it that had nothing to do with friendship but rather suggested distant patronage; snow fell softly, like forgetfulness, and sharply, like ill-luck; . . .

IV

[Baird continued to pay attention to Christina and made a favourable impression on the girl, whose mind had perhaps been prepared by the words of the gipsy woman at the Martinmas Fair. Spring came at last. The *Sirius* had now been refitted and loaded with timber for Australia, and both Christina and her father were prepared for further developments. Baird was proud of his ship, particularly of her figure-head, and when he invited them to look over the *Sirius* they agreed to do so. No doubt he met them at the gangway.]

"You see they didn't forget her figurehead when they were building her" he said.

His companions followed him obediently to the bows and, looking up, were silent. Lummie, because he did not know what to say. He was most willing to take Baird's word for its fineness though it appeared to him mainly as a mass of extraordinary huge and unfamiliar contours; size, always likely to appal Christina, appalled her here, for the great torso that reared itself high above the horizontal line of the quay was awe-inspiring because of its human shape, because of a terrific solidity which held suggestion of latent violence in the sharp, arresting outline; it made her shudder. Perhaps she had never before realized the importance of Baird. That he was in absolute command of living men on errands involving great profits and losses, and carried out between the snarling teeth of the powers of nature for weeks and months at a stretch, had never come home to her. Life, death, risk, a responsibility, more direct and pressing than almost any other in the world; she had realised none of these. She did not realise them now but her awe of the inanimate presence towering above her extended itself in some measure to her suitor—for she now believed him to be that—and gave him a more important place in her mind.

The man who designed the figurehead of the *Sirius* had been proud of his work. He had set the ruler of the dog-star with his arms folded across his broad breast that would meet the forefront onslaught of the seas, his head thrown back into a crown of stars. Below the scroll work from which his loins rose was a couchant greyhound.

They went up the gangway and stood on deck. Father and daughter looked round rather shyly.

"Come below," said Baird, leading the way down the companion from which the smell of new paint was mingling with the salt air.

There had been a great scrub-out on the foregoing day and all traces of workmen had vanished. They descended into the mellow darkness and Christina, who had not dreamed that a ship could feel so solid underfoot, let her wondering eyes roam over the new red Utrecht velvet and rich brown teak of the saloon. No detail of comfort was lacking; an ornamental clock presented to Baird in Australia was screwed above the moulded sideboard and a gold embroidered Indian shawl had been laid as a cloth over the polished dining-table. The skipper had put a few of his possessions obout the opulent upholstery of his own cabin to add to the effect he desired. Christina looked curiously at the bunk covered with a fur rug. She had supposed that all sailors slept in hammocks.

There were a couple of bottles of good sherry awaiting the guests and a cake for Christina. She admired the neat way he had cut it and set it out with the glasses on the costly Oriental fabric.

"You must come back again when I'm living on board and have a steward to wait on you," said he, as he poured out the wine, "I shall be here a while before we sail."

"No use paying for lodgings when you've such a place as this," observed Mill.

"And what do _you_ think of it, Miss?"

"It's not very like what I expected."

"Better or worse—eh?"

"Oh, far better!" said Christina, growing a little pink.

Baird leaned back in his chair and looked at her from under his thick, short eyelashes. He laughted loudly. Her timidity pleased him and he was gratified by her approval.

"Did you think I berthed in the fo'csle?" he exclaimed. She turned scarlet, embarrassed by his laugh and the unfamiliar words.

"Oh, no offence meant," he said quickly, alarmed lest he should have estranged her. "I've no business to use sailors' talk to a lady. I'm forgetting my manners and I expect I've got too proud to remember them because I've superintended all this myself. I've had a free hand and no expense spared."

The excellent sherry had stirred up Lummie's natural infelicity of speech.

"You're a silly girl, Christina," said he, leaning across the table. "Here we are, entertained by the Captain and favoured with a sight of his ship. You should know better than to be so silly."

Though he did not speak with real harshness, her lips trembled. Baird was a past master, when he liked, in representing himself agreeably.

15

"I like a lady to *be* a lady," he said, looking very straight at Mill, "and I'm all with Miss Christina, and that's the truth, Sir. My uncle was at sea and my aunt often went with him but I've heard him say that he never allowed a nautical word at table so long as she was there. You'll excuse my freedom, but I'd take Miss Christina's taste before anyone else's, if I may say so."

It was Lummie's turn to be out of countenance and he was much impressed. He had not known in the least what he was blaming his daughter for; he had only gathered that the skipper was apologising for something and he had taken for granted that it was unnecessary. He murmured in a propitiating way. Christina's heart beat. He was a wonderful man, their host. For all her set ways, she had no conceit and she was astonished to find that he could value her opinion so highly. She thought of it a good deal and after she got home she stayed some time in her room in the dusk considering the little incident as if it had happened to somebody else.

When Baird had seen his guests home he returned to the ship and he also sat thinking in the saloon. Lummie had not drunk much sherry and the captain poured out and emptied glass after glass. He was no drinker, as drinkers went in those days, but the wine helped to develop the satisfaction in him.

He now believed that Christina would accept him and he was pleased with the way he had turned her little embarrassment to account; it was one of those lucky strokes that he made sometimes. He twirled the wineglass in his fingers and remembered how Mill's jaw had dropped as he rounded on him and the honest freedom of his own words—just what was wanted to take the fancy of a bread and butter Miss. How could she know that any man might deal anyhow with the like of her father? Some of his own dealing with those who got in his way—or who thought they were going to—came back to him pleasantly. How well he went down with his fellow creatures! He was by no means the sea-bully dear to fiction, yet those to whom he was most acceptable were apt to be landsmen. There was little need on land for the rough side of himself to compel the attention he wished to have in the world, for he realised very well that his virile appeal disposed it in his favour.

That evening Ann Wishart had a description of the visit to the *Sirius* with its main points left out. Though Christina had been wont to discuss every word spoken by Aeneas Halket with her, she said little about Baird. Nor could Ann, who was well versed in the gossip of the place and had been asked when the wedding at Lummie Mill's was to be, get anything from her. It was this silence on Christina's part which led to the opening of her father's eyes.

Lummie had seen nothing in the skipper but a desirable acquaintance with whom to interchange the small amenities he loved. He was really sorry the time was coming when Baird would go to sea again and be no more at hand to stroll with him on the links when the Bank of Angus was shut. He had never considered him in relation to his daughter.

Ann had long burned with curiosity. Her contempt for sailors had abated where Baird was concerned. He had cut a great figure in the town and the firm of Torrie, Gibson and Hunter, whose man he was, took a high place in the world of commercial shipping. Whether he went to sea again after his next voyage or whether, as rumour had it, he would retire, she could imagine Christina installed in one of those new houses—some of which had even carriage drives—and taking a position to match her setting.

It was Ann's habit to attend, personally, to the hearth of Mill's study. The evening had grown chilly at sundown and she found him with his slippered feet on the fender. The fire lacked nothing but she began to use the poker.

Mill was always ready for a word with anybody.

"We've had a visit to Captain Baird's ship", he began.

"Aye, I kent ye was there. I could believe it was a grand ship."

"Cake and wine for us. Nothing spared."

She tossed her head.

"I wid believe that too. He'd be thinkin' naething guid eneuch for Miss Christina."

"Yes, Oh yes," said Lummie with his little gratified squeak. "He's a very polite man, the Captain."

She could almost have choked him for his innocence.

"He's lucky", she observed, grimly.

"Quite, quite. He had all the money he required for the furnishing. A fine rug on his bed too; I forget the name of the fur though he told me he'd got it in a present when he was in America."

Ann saw that a bombshell was needed, but she was a woman of action.

"And ye'll be no sparin' expense yersel, I doot, for the weddin' ".

"The wedding—?"

He looked up at the tight spare figure and at length her meaning dawned on him.

"Oh dear me," he exclaimed, "dear, dear me! But surely—"

"Aw—" breathed Ann, slowly, closing her eyes and drawing her lips back from her prominent gums in a smile of ineffable knowledge, "it's easy seen—"

"But—" He began again.

"I'll need tae be gangin' ", she broke in. "The roast's on the jack and Eliza's awa' oot".

It was two days after this that Baird formally asked Mill for permission to pay his addresses to Christina and that Mill replied, "Of course, of course," with the responsiveness of a door bell to the hand of a caller. A small seizure of politeness had ripped the words from him; also there was an idea at the back of his mind that should he wish to do so, he could still direct Christina to refuse before there was time for a proposal. But Baird, thanking him warmly for his consent departed, leaving him a good deal fussed. As the skipper walked upstairs without further ado and asked Christina to marry him there was no opportunity for parental advice.

Mill stood bewildered below. He had expected to hear the front door shut; what he did hear was the sound of Baird's voice in the drawingroom above. He had not realised enough to go up and protest against this unauthorised haste, nor was he really certain of which way he wished the matter to turn.

While Baird declared his love, Christina was standing with her back to the window almost as much disturbed as her father, but getting over it as the scene she had been led to look on as a possibility enacted itself. Andrew Baird had never made an honourable proposal to a woman in his life, and to anyone understanding the whole truth about the situation, there might have been a lurking humour in the fact that the skipper, knowing as little about it as the girl did, conceived the same procedure to be necessary. He went down on one knee and the sight hypnotised the spectator that was in Christina. Her vision was coming true and it was a wonderful thing to realise that she was, indeed, playing a part in the romantic drama, suspected, shadowed, that lay outside her placid life. It was a sense of the fitness of things which made her turn away and say in her quiet voice,

"It is very kind of you but I must take a day or two to think about it."

She had turned it over in her mind a good deal in the last week. She had not liked to speak of it to her father, feeling that it was not her place to suggest such a thing as a love affair. Only to Ann, had she ever hinted the possibility of marriage and that in a remote disembodied manner.

"Mr Mill has given me his word he will consent. All I need now is for you to say you'll take me," said Baird.

A wave of relief went over her to think there was no necessity to broach the subject to her father.

"You mustn't say 'no'," said Baird. "You won't do that."

She had stepped back and he caught her hand. It lay in his like something inanimate. She was a little flustered by the strong grip but the sensation of his taking her into the more important half of womankind obsessed her. He made as though to draw her to him but the startled look that came into her eyes caused him to refrain. He must risk nothing, and he imagined that all honest women saw fit to behave in the same way at first whatever they might do afterwards. Of course she was acting a comedy. In a measure he was quite right, for she was absorbed in the part that circumstances had given her; yet he had never been further from understanding her than at that moment.

"You'll make up your mind the right way tomorrow," said he. "I shall come back the next day and you won't refuse. Mind, I have your father's word that he'll consent."

"Oh, I am quite pleased," faltered she.

Lummie, who had recovered his wits, opened the door and stood looking at them.

Baird was at a loss for a minute. There was a flat silence. At times, the most simple people do the right thing from sheer simplicity and it was Christina who gave the death-blow to the uncomfortable moment.

"Goodbye, Captain Baird," she said, putting out her hand again. Baird laid hold of it as though it had been a tow-rope and then left the room.

"I'll be back the day after tomorrow," he said again as he went.

"What's that he was saying about the day after tomorrow?" enquired Mill, after he had gone.

"He said he was coming back, Papa."

"I suppose he was telling you some nonsense about being in love with you?"

Though he had no real objection to the engagement and though, since his enlightenment by Ann, he was inclined to think well of it, this seemed to him the legitimate way of approaching the subject. It was the custom of his time.

"He was asking me to marry him."

"And what did you say to it, Christina?"

"I said I would think about it."

Her calm lack of enthusiasm at once revealed his true wishes to him.

"You might be throwing away a good chance. D'ye like him, Christina?"

"Yes, I like him well enough."

"You might do worse. My bit of money—it's more than you might think too—will go to you and with what he makes, you'll be well set up. Torrie, Gibson and Hunter are not likely to let him go."

There was no word about love from either of them. To Mill, love meant the bygone shadow of a slight thing and Christina took it to be identical with marriage. But she was proud to be chosen by Baird and the remembrance of his championship on board the *Sirius* was a secret pleasure, something like the picture of St Cecilia had once been. She was happy and two thoughts were mixed in her mind in an agreeable manner; that of Baird on one knee and the words of her acquaintance with the red and green brushes. She had said, "Ye should get a man that'll gie ye a sicht o' the world."

The engagement rolled over the house like an incoming tide. Mill talked about nothing else, Christina said little, but Ann made up for her lack of words with the plenitude of her own. The girl was lost in the effort of realising her new circumstances. She had no misgivings about the changes which must come to all her ways of life. Having taken prosperity for granted in the placidity of home, lacking nothing, disturbed by nothing, at ease and contented for nearly twenty-seven years, she could not imagine that fortune could play her false; anything so outrageous could never happen. She did not reassure herself, having no need of reassurance. She was so young in some ways, so old in others, having nothing of the high spirits of youth, none of its rebellions or aspirations but all and more than its inexperience. The only progressive stir that had ever touched her had been set going by the woman with the brooms.

And now, she enjoyed her added importance. Ann, once the engagement was a fact, went over to the captain, horse and foot, for she admired him as an adjunct to the family. To Christina, he was mainly a guarantee of security and consideration from whose protection she would look tranquilly on the novelties of a world she did not know.

The town could hardly believe its ears when it heard that Baird was to take his bride with him on the approaching voyage and that they were to be married on the day they sailed. It had cost him a deal of talking to get this decided but he was a good talker and Mill gave in after a half-hearted resistance. Time was getting on, there were settlements to be made and the wedding outfit to be completed. There would be little space for a honeymoon. Baird put it to Mill that it would be a hard case for a man to leave his new-made wife and go off at once on an Australian voyage. There was every comfort on board the *Sirius* and his last steward, who was signing on again, had a daughter who could be engaged and taken with them to wait on the captain's wife. At Adelaide, where he had a large acquaintance, Christina would be a woman of standing. How often she had listened to his big accounts of the fine town and gay company and the hospitable houses of the shipowners and their friends. She told herself that she would see all this from her vantage point behind her travelled husband. And, before all, was she not herself—Christina—safe and hedged by the consideration of those around her from the rough things that might happen to the less favoured? And now that she had been inside a ship, and felt how big and solid it was, she could well believe what Baird had said about its safety.

Lummie did not write the news to his sister Isabella until the matter was settled in detail; he did not know how far she would approve the notion of Christina being whisked off to such a distance. But he had no mind to be in the line of fire between Isabella and the skipper so he waited till the wedding day was settled and the matter clinched by publicity before writing to her himself or letting Christina do so. Things went quickly where Andrew Baird was concerned so it was a week after that "day after tomorrow" when he returned for his answer that Mrs Halket learned of the engagement. Had Lummie seen her lay down his letter he would have been reassured. She looked out of her window on to the unpretentious street—so sad a contrast to Gayfield Square—and a slow smile crept to her lips. She saw herself presiding over the house in the Bow Butts; even, at last, with Ann Wishart. It was for the best for everybody. Christina was nearly twenty-seven and though Isabella had once fancied that her stepson was attracted by her, she had evidently been mistaken, for Aeneas, whose business was now keeping him a good deal abroad, had made no special effort to see the girl when he came home. She wrote to congratulate her niece and suggested that she should help her to get her wedding clothes. The stars in their courses fought for Baird, as they do for most thrusters.

Though the skipper's courtship had been begun for a variety of reasons, many of which had little to do with love, his fancy, in some measure, had been caught. He did not want a wife with a vivid personality who might be likely to get into mischief whilst he was at sea; he wanted a woman a little superior to himself socially. He came of a family whose members were no rovers at heart, and who, though they had one seaman among them, were far from pleased by the production of a second. He had flown in their faces by his choice of a profession but there was enough of the hereditary smug instinct of worldly advancement in him to make him desire a wife who dressed richly and had the air of being apart from the herd of everyday. Christina was an only child, daughter of a man who had something to leave. And, beyond that, her intense femininity pleased him, the rustle of her silk skirt, the thin shoe on her pointed foot; he admired her white fingers too as Aeneas had done, but not with the same knowledge. He liked them to be white because they looked as if they did not work but the unusual beauty of their shape was a subtlety beyond him. She was not clever or accomplished but men married their wives for convenience mainly, and were lucky if they got any attraction thrown in. He found enough of that in Christina to make a voyage with her pleasant while the novelty lasted; and when he brought her home and settled her in a handsome house he would not be likely to take her to sea again and he would be able to live his own life, unmolested on one side of the world and a very reputable one on the other. And there would be a good deal less of the latter than of the former.

He had had a universal success with the women he had admired and he would have been much surprised if Christina had rejected him. No doubt she was glad enough to get away from her old ninny of a father, he told himself, though to see her stiff ways with a lover she did not wish you to suppose it. He smiled, thinking of her pretences; he would soon knock them out of her and she would like him all the better for it. In any case he would weary of her sooner or later but the advantages which had influenced him would still be left. And meantime he liked her well enough.

Spring is late in Scotland, but this year it arrived unusually early, and, on Christina's wedding day, it was bright and the sun warm. The town was hugely interested in the event and Lummie's guests were dressed in their best. The ceremony would take place in the drawing room and in the dining room below the table was laid for wedding "breakfast".

A crowd of the humbler townsfolk were gathered in the Bow Butts, agog to see the company arriving, though the real sight would be when Captain Baird and his bride drove down to the harbour from which the *Sirius*—now covered with bunting—would be tugged out to sea. Inside the house Mrs Halket and Ann, united for once, attired Christina in the white finery and bridal wreath which had cost them so much thought.

Christina herself was calm and smiling. As the couple stood before the minister she thought again of the woman on the links; she would have liked to be able to tell her that she was taking her advice. She sat through

22

the wedding feast listening to the speeches and healths and congratula-
tions and heard her husband assuring his friends that this was the
happiest day of his life. Baird liked wine as much as anyone but he knew
that he had to keep his head clear and get out to sea triumphantly in the
face of half the town and he drank little; the two distant relations of the
bride, an elderly brother and sister, were very favourably impressed by
him.

"You have got a fine man," said the old lady. "See that you value him,
my dear. Such a chance never came my way."

Christina wondered if this was the happiest day of her life and she
supposed it was. She was sorry to leave home and her father and she
wished Ann were coming with her. For one minute fear of the unknown
sprang up in her—only for one minute. Surely she had got the strongest
protector anyone could desire and he loved her. Some day, when he was
away at sea she would come home again and stay in the familiar house.
She could not feel she was leaving for good and all.

By four o'clock the Bow Butts was crowded again, for the open
carriage, hired for the occasion, was at the gate; the bridegroom had
insisted that grey horses were to be got somehow, and a very creditable
pair were produced. There was a bunch of white ribbons on the whip,
and the boy who came in to clean the knives had tied an old shoe to the
axle above which they sat. When they started the crowd hurried after
them to the harbour.

Ferry Street was thick with people: the ships' chandlers and other
small provision merchants left their shops to take care of themselves
whilst they made for the quay. Half way down the street, where the
model of a sailing ship projected from the upper storey a knot of sailors
and fishermen raised a shout as the carriage passed which was taken up
further on. Women stood in their doors looking after it, keeping their
mouths open and their eyes screwed up as all inhabitants of east coast
Scottish towns seem to do at the passage of anything arresting. The
younger women followed their neighbours to see the end of the show
and the old ones peeping round the sides of their doorways enchange
comments with each other.

"Aye, Miss Lummie Mill," said one. "She's a denty thing tae be awa' till
Austrailly wi' a caird like yon."

"Ah, I mind her when she was a wee thing wi' a tow-heid," said
another.

"What'll Lummie dae the noo, puir stock? He'll hae tae get a wife,
himsel!"

"Fie!—*him*? Wha'd hae Lummie?"

"No me!" exclaimed a woman over eighty. "Baird's the lad I'd tak."

Meanwhile the couple stood on the quay. The *Sirius* lay in the strait with the tug in attendance.

To the new-made wife of the Captain the ship looked smaller than when she had stared up at her bows a few weeks ago. Mill and his sister and the guests who were arriving in twos and threes, pressed round them and spectators from the town grew in number every minute. One of the *Sirius's* boats was rising and falling almost imperceptibly with the scarcely moving water at the foot of the landing steps; now and then a ripple from nowhere made little licking sounds about the steps fringed with fine pieces of weed. Across the watermouth below the fishing village and divided from there by the River Esk merging itself in the salt water estuary, the reflections of the stone houses and whitewashed walls with the little kirk up the rising ground were mirrored upside down.

Ann Wishart was sniffling and Lummie's nervous hilarity had stopped. Baird took off his hat and held out his hand to his father-in-law; people crowded about him, wishing him prosperity and health and wealth and everything they could think of.

Christina bade goodbye to Mrs Halket and Ann and, almost for the first time in her life, put her arms around her father's neck. The tears were in her eyes. She could hardly see as Baird handed her down the steps and into the boat where a red cushion awaited her. Then they were sliding along the surface of the oily water.

The party ashore watched them reach the ship and stand on deck together, a dark figure and a light one with a floating veil. The boat ran up the davits.

The sound of voices and a shouted order or two came across and in a few minutes the tug drew into line ahead of the ship and the centre of the half submerged tow-rope rose to form a taut line with the ends; there was a churning of water and they were moving. Baird had disappeared and the cheer from the quay came to Christina over the sound of thrashing paddles. Looking back, she could distinguish for a long time above the waving handkerchiefs her father's tall hat held high over his head.

She had no suspicion of its celebrity.

V

It was on the second afternoon since they had sailed that Christina Baird sat in the shelter of the midshiphouse, her eyes on the sullen horizon of grey water between which and herself there burst out an occasional bar of ragged white; morning had dawned to a falling glass that by midday had dropped and was dropping lower and lower. She was very cold in spite of her thick cloak; but though they were beginning to roll a good deal she had not felt seasick. Like many tenderly nurtured people she was proving a good sailor. But the growing instability of the deck and the sudden periodical shocks that were going through the *Sirius* in answer to some unseen force were but one of her troubles. A loneliness and a lostness such as she had never dreamed of in her sheltered life were on her. She would catch her breath and tears would rise at the thought of the house she had left only the day before yesterday; of Ann in her safe, warm kitchen and her father with his newspaper in the evenings.

She had seen nothing of Baird all day and she knew him to be busied with the mysteries of his profession. For this she was deeply grateful. It had been one of his favourite theories that all women were alike and Christina's terrified recoil from his love-making was proving him to be wrong. He was exasperated by her and had sworn at her in his contemptuous wrath and to the girl, who had never heard a word of profanity nearer than a distant corner of a street, the mildest oath seemed a branding crime. He had never supposed such a woman to exist and today he had not so much as inquired whether she were sick or well, dry or drenched, or whether she had found a corner to protect her from the seas that were getting up in the chill of the shifting grey world around them. He knew by the barometer and the look of things that he might soon have his hands full. He would be glad to forget her; idiot that she was. He had come to no meal and she had tried to eat the food the steward brought her as she sat alone with Baird's empty chair screwed to the floor at the other side of the saloon table. The steward had found her a cloak and a sheltered corner. He was a kind man and had told her that the Captain would soon be along to look after her and that the first days out were always busy ones with him. She had thanked him faintly, understanding his desire to be kind; but Baird's absence was welcome; she found his anger and his love-making equally dreadful. The girl who was her maid watched her, wondering, from the head of the companion. She had been born by the sea and lived among its followers and the voyage was much to her taste. She pitied the young lady down whose cheek she had more than once seen the homesick tears drip in the forty-eight hours they had been out. Both she and her father had asked her if she would not be better in her cabin and had been answered by a shake of the head.

At sunset, a bank of cloud low in the south-east was feeling its way along the horizon and the sun's vanishing presence could be guessed rather than seen through the thickness that invaded the west. They had begun to pitch and the shocks under Christina's feet were coming at shorter intervals; each one brought a dull, thudding bang that spent itself in the white line of stinging foam that drove, hissing, to starboard from under the ship. Suddenly a splash of water leaped over the side, spouting like a fountain, and in spite of her preoccupation an acute start of dismay took her. There was another bang and a seething hiss; a scream of wind flew somewhere overhead. She was aware that her feet were drenched. She gripped the arms of her chair and tried to get up. But the deck rose in front of her and she sat down, her eyes staring. It was getting dark and through the livid colour that had fallen on the world Baird came tramping round on her. He was in oilskins and looked unfamiliar and uncouth with the wet shining on him. Before she could speak he had snatched her arm and was dragging her from her seat. She clung to him frantically as the deck rose again.

"What are you doing here?" he shouted. "Do you think I'm going to put down a boat for every fool that's whipped overboard? Get down, I tell you! You'll be glad enough to be in your bunk in an hour or two."

There was a whirling rose in the rigging as he held her at the top of the companion and shouted for the steward. The man came up and he thrust her into his arms, cursing both him and his daughter for leaving her so long on deck. The girl and her father, holding to everything they could reach, supported Christina till they got her below and into her cabin. The glass was still dropping.

"See and get her beddit, Maggie, and I'll awa' and seek a drappie whisky till her," said the steward.

Maggie took off Christina's dress and her soaked stockings and covered her with blankets in her berth. Her arm ached from Baird's grip and she was frightened and dazed by his rough grasp and angry words; but now the physical fear that grew on her as they went into the weather that came to meet them was obliterating everything else.

March had come in and gone out like a lamb and April had worn a face that was falsely bright. That lying spring month was to be paid for her lies and the North Sea was going to help to pay her.

As the hours went by the gale increased and in the lulls of its unholy yelling, Christina could hear the scudding of bare feet above and a stir that made her heart sink. She did not know what was happening— perhaps they were going down—perhaps they were getting out the boats; she lay cowering, using all her strength not to be thrown on the floor. She had told Maggie to leave her, but since Maggie had gone, every moment was laden with greater dread. She could distinguish occasional wafts of men's shouting and once she heard Baird's voice of brass above the bewilderment of banging and swinging. One or two crashes of crockery came to her ears. The cabin was a large one, as the cabins of sailing ships went, but they were battened down now, and closed ports let in little air. The rocking and plunging grew more and more violent and every moveable object begun to slide across the drugget, to be shot back again and merged with others till a fresh pitch scattered the wedge anew. She lay clinging to the bracket of a little shelf beside her. Had she been seasick she would have suffered less, mentally, but she had not even a headache to take her thoughts from the anguish of fear.

At eight o'clock Maggie wormed and thrust her way through the door and stood precariously over her with a metal bowl containing a piece of toast.

"A was bringing ye a puckle soup," she was saying into her ear," but it wadna bide intill the bowl. It was awa' afore A could win till ye."

"Stay with me," begged Christina, "Don't go away and leave me."

The girl sat down on the floor holding onto the edge of the bunk, for she could hardly stand, but she managed to secure Christina's little trunk in a corner so that it should not roll on the top of them. She wondered what was the matter with the lady who seemed in no danger of seasickness.

"Ye're no feared are ye, Mistress Baird?" she enquired at at last.

"Oh, I am, I am."

"But ye'll no need to fleg yersel'. The sea's a bittie coorse, whiles, but ye need na mak' ado about that. A'm no feared, ye see."

"Is that true? Are you not?" whispered Christina.

"Na, na."

Maggie spoke stoutly but she was not really happy; she had never been on a long voyage, though she had spent some hours at a time on fishing smacks. She had hailed the notion of going all the way to Australia with the Captain's lady. But such noise of wind and water awed her and all the medley of sounds that go on in a windjammer in bad weather were increasing with every plunge. To Christina there was no awe; the

27

imminent heartbreaking fear of death was with her and nothing else. She could scarcely distinguish one thing from another. All was merged into the blackness of terror. Cries like the voices of dying fiends, twanged and battled in the rigging. The ship groaned and creaked. Sometimes she seemed to sink as though she must long since have left the surface of the ocean under the thuds and blows that assailed her. The scudding of feet above Christina's head would be swallowed by the roar that enveloped everything.

The two young women spoke no more as the hours dragged by. They could not have heard each others' voices. In one of their dizzying plunges their lamp went out and the dark closed in on them. Towards the small hours of the morning at a turn of the wind, the seas began to strike the ship's bell and spasms of ringing were sharp above the pandemonium of the storm and the pounding and rattling as the water thrashed the deck Then, in the midst of it all the malign elements pounced on them, a hundred and a thousandfold strong, and side by side, they clung together in what seemed to them to be the very breaking up of the universe. What they had gone through was as nothing compared to what swooped upon them before dawn of that chill April morning; now they were tossed as to the skies, now cast down to bottomlessness. In the dark they were blind and their hearing grew more acute for the different sounds contending together. It seemed to their quickened ears that nothing could survive and no plank hold. The *Sirius* was thrown, bashed, hurled in the trough of the seas. There were no more scudding feet. Only the ship's bell punctuating chaos with its crazy and tormented tongue.

Just before sunrise the wind dropped and the sea began to go down.

In the pale light Maggie went out to see what remained to be seen after such a night; she was able to stand now and she made her way to the saloon where she found her father setting out coffee for Captain Baird. She took a cupful for Christina and having coaxed her to swallow it, she set to work to clear the cabin of the things strewn about it, for the slow swell that the sea's fury had left behind did not hinder her movements much.

When she came back from her own meal she brought news of the night's damage. They had lost two boats; the side of the galley was stove in and the second mate had been dashed against the angle of a locker and his leg was broken. They were going to put in to Leith that night.

"Aye, the Captain's no very pleased tae be gangin' in," said Maggie, "but ye ken yon lad's mither—she's a widdy that was married upon Maister

Torrie, Martinmas last—wad gar her man skirl gin aucht gae'd wrang wi' him. Syne it wadna dae tae let him want the doctor."

There was no persuading her mistress to go on deck now. Christina lay, thankful to be quiet. She had washed her tearstained face and Maggie had brushed her hair. Too tired to give way to grief, she asked nothing of the girl but that she would stay beside her.

A drizzling rain had come on that was sprinkling the face of the quieted sea and in the watery light showing through the port she fell into the dreamless dead sleep of exhaustion. At last her maid stole quietly to her side and, after listening to her regular breathing, went on tiptoe out of the cabin. When she looked in again all was still. In the afternoon she returned with food and laid her hand on her to wake her; Christina waved her away.

"Let me sleep," she murmured.

"I'd no let onybody disturb ye till ye cry on me," said Maggie who was longing for repose on her own account.

"Oh yes—thank you," sighed Christina, turning over into the oblivion from which she had scarcely emerged.

It was almost dark when the fathomless sleep of utter fatigue began to wear thin, like a garment, and Christina awoke with a start. She could not imagine where she was. Then, drop by drop, realisation came back in such a tumult that it was a few moments before she became aware that they were not moving. The cabin floor was as still as pavement. What new terror was this? She sat up, her hands pressed together. There was a sound of hammering that echoed in a curious way as though flung across a wide space of silence. Everything else was quiet except for an occasional casual voice. There was that blank dumb suggestion of suspended animation round her which pervades the cabin of a stationary ship. Her heart leaped in her and she sprang to the port hole. They were lying in Leith Dock.

Baird had decided that the second mate must be landed and for the better accomplishment of this they lay alongside the wharf where Torrie Gibson and Hunter had their warehouses and offices. He had gone ashore to find the firm's Edinburgh agent and send word to Torrie of his stepson's mishap; also he meant to get extra help and work all night on the repairing begun already on board so as to get out, if possible, on the next afternoon's tide. He would have to see the young fellow disposed where he could be attended to and that might take time. There was a black look on Baird's face. He was exasperated by the delay, by the damage to the ship, by the clumsiness of Torrie's stepson who had been ass enough to get himself injured at the very start of the voyage and must be replaced; by the woman he had neither seen nor heard of since he had thrust her into the steward's arms at the head of the companion.

What kind of life was he going to have with such a bargain as he had saddled himself with? He had imagined that he had done well for himself and her money was all right of course but now he had to sail all the way to Australia and back with a woman who seemed to be no more than a useless encumbrance, who had repulsed his every advance to her with sulks and tears. Thank God, he could leave her ashore once they were at home again. She was not worth troubling about and there were plenty of women where they were going who were. Let her stay in her cabin and sulk to her heart's content. He thrust her out of his mind; he had other things to do than bother about her. He would have a square meal ashore that would do him good after the strain and racket of the last twenty-four hours.

Christina stole to the door and opened it. All was quiet. She had lain down half-dressed that morning but she went back for her cloak and, wrapping herself in it, crept up the companion steps and peered round. A steady rain was falling and making pools of mud on the wharf. In the dim, lowering light she could see that the gangway was down. She stood holding her breath Supposing —!

She turned and went down to her cabin, shaking all over and trying to calm herself—here—now—was a chance! She did not know how soon Maggie might come back. Maggie was a good, kind girl—

She dressed herself as quickly as she could with her trembling fingers. For the first time in her life she was nerving herself for an effort. Terror can do strange things. Her fears sprang upon her like leaping dogs but she held them down with all her force. Anything that could happen to her must be better than those desperate experiences and she might have to live through others of the same sort. The idea nerved her. She put all her money in her pocket and drew her cloak more closely around her.

She could never afterwards remember how she got on deck. That shutting of the door behind her began a blank of sickening apprehension, but she knew that her husband would be away, from something Maggie had said, and she saw that though there were men moving about the fore part of the ship, the short distance between them and her goal was empty. She would have waited till it was quite dark but for Maggie's possible appearance at any minute. There were a few scattered figures a little way along the quay and she had sense to know that she must not run while they were anywhere in sight. If she kept her head and went slowly casual loiterers might pay her nothing but a passing heed; the terror that had been able to rouse her to action made her take any risk sooner than delay for a moment; there was not only the voyage across the world but its return journey on that frightful sea.

She slipped like a shadow to the gangway and crossed it, too terrified to send a glance towards the fo'csle where the hammering was going on.

In the darkness of a shed she stood to regain her dazed wits. She was prepared to run if she was observed till she fell dead. But hammering went on and the voices in the fo'csle. She was crying from the reaction of her effort but she checked her tears and began to slip like a hunted cat among the shanties and wood piles and varied buildings in the direction of the lighted houses. She did not know where she was going except that it was inland, away from the ship.

When she emerged into a wide cobble-stoned place her fears, dulled for a space by her success, beset her again. But the sparse oil lamps, blurred by the wet, threw so little light that she was swallowed up by the grey of the east-coast evening. Fear of the sea and fear of discovery abating, she begun to fear her own lostness in this world of dark, grimy little streets and rough-looking strangers.

She knew that she must speak to somebody if she was to find her way to Edinburgh, for it was her Aunt Halket's house that she was counting on for a refuge. It was a desperate policy for she was ignorant of whether Baird knew Mrs Halket's address. She thought he did not. But, once behind its walls, no power should drag her to the ship again. Surely, surely there would be someone who would pity her and get her home. And Andrew Baird would be gone—far on the other side of the world.

The rain came down, increasing from a steady fall to a deluge. The causeys ran like rivers and the onslaught of drops beat up from the cobbles and chilled her feet through her thin boots. Her cloak was sopped and her ankles icy cold; her voluminous skirt, which she tried to hold up, grew heavy with the leaden wet. She stopped, dismayed, by a little house at whose firelit window, about the height of her elbow from the ground, there was the dark outline of a figure staring at her from the inner side of the pane. Then it was gone and the window all light. Some one opened the door, beckoning. There was a step down from its threshold and she nearly stumbled in as a kindly hand drew her in.

"Lordsakes!" a small, square woman was saying. "Sic a night for a leddy to be oot! Come in-by to the fire. Aw dear—aye, sic a nicht!"

31

The exclamations were due to the sight of Christina's fine poplin skirt bordered with grimy mud.

She led her to the fire and a man in a deal chair in front of it pulled aside to give her room, looking at her with astonishment, pipe in hand.

She started back. It seemed to her distracted mind and overstrained nerves that she must have reached the end of her journey and landed amongst savages. The man was quite black.

The square woman laughed.

"Na, na, ye need'na be feared!" She exclaimed, clapping her protectingly on the shoulder, "He'll no hurt ye. He's the sweep, ye ken. Sit doon, puir thing, and I'll mak' ye a cuppie tea."

"You're so kind," said Christina, faintly, "and I've lost my way."

She sat down and warmed her feet, water dripping from her on to the hearthstone. The woman took a kettle and went into the scullery. A clock ticked steadily and after a little it wheezed and struck eight.

"And whaur are ye for?" asked the sweep, who had not yet spoken.

"I want to go to Edinburgh. My aunt lives there," replied Christina, her eyes filling again.

"Dod, ye'll no can walk."

"No, I can't. If I could only hire a carriage! Do you think I could get one anywhere? I've got a lot of money?" she added, naively.

At such an unusual statement the woman came out of the scullery. Husband and wife considered her from head to foot.

"Ye'd maybe get a machine from the Black Horse," said the wife, recovering first.

The sweep remained speechless. Never had he met anybody who made such a claim.

"I will give you ten shillings if you will get me a carriage that I can go to Edinburgh in."

There was another awed silence. The woman's kind heart had made her take in this dripping bird of passage but her thrifty mind must have its turn now.

"Awa wi' ye, Geordie, to the Black Horse!" she exclaimed, briskly.

He hesitated, got up and took his hat from a peg. As he opened the door the rain drove in. A gleam of humour came into his eye.

"Aweel, A'm needin' a wash," said he as he stepped out.

Christina sipped her tea nervously, for now that the prospect had improved, she was in an agony to get on. She was determined not to say she had come from the ship, lest some rumour of her flight should reach the dock and it was not easy to evade the woman's questions. She did not know how far inland she had come. It seemed like miles. The rain had almost stopped when the immense shadow of a rickety hood darkened the window and the sweep, whose face was beginning to look like the map of a hilly country, came back with it.

She thanked the couple profusely and, having produced a ten-shilling bit from her purse, climbed in and shrank back as far as she could into the recesses of her new-found shelter.

"Whaur'll she be gangin' till?" asked the driver of the sweep, as Christina did not speak.

"Oh, please tell him 41 Niven Street," she said, collecting her wits.

"I dinna ken whaur that'll be," said the driver, "Will't be i' the Auld Toon?"

"It's by Barbados Place, aside the Kirk," said the sweep. "Noo then, awa ye go." They trotted slowly away.

Christina was very cold in spite of the hot tea she had swallowed and by the time they had traversed interminally through the wretched evening and were getting into the Edinburgh streets she was aching from the jolting over ill-kept roads. At the end of the journey she got out feasting her eyes on the sanctuary of a familiar place and rang the bell. The door opened, but where she had expected to meet her aunt's maid-servant she found Aeneas Halket.

The overwhelming surprise upset what composure she had gained in her solitary drive and she almost thrust herself against him, crying, "Let me in! Let me in!"

Aeneas was staggered. He drew her into the little hall and she sat down on a bench, a dishevelled, muddied figure. Her boots made damp marks on the stone.

"Where have you come from? What's the matter?" he exclaimed. "What has happened?"

The driver had left his perch. He was hammering at the door. He wanted to be paid. Christina sought her purse and gave it to Aeneas.

"I daren't go out—pay him, please! Give him anything he asks, only tell him to say nothing about me. Be sure you tell him to say nothing!" she sobbed.

When the man had gone Aeneas brought her into the room he had been sitting in. It was warm and lighted.

"Why are you here?" she asked him.

He smiled, thinking the question might have come more fittingly from himself.

"I came from France yesterday. My stepmother is away."

Then he stopped, remembering that Mrs Halket had gone to Christina's wedding.

"But what is the matter? Where is Captain Baird?"

She turned a shade paler.

"Promise me that you will let nobody know I am here—*promise!*" She began to cry hysterically.

He was so dumbfounded that no word of pity for her plight had come from him.

"Don't cry, don't cry like that," he said at last, putting his hand on her shoulder. She wept on, but more quietly.

"Tell me," he said again. "You *must* tell me what's the matter. I heard you were to sail with Captain Baird, but what can have happened? Have they left you behind?"

A step sounded on the pavement outside and she clasped her hands, her eyes wide, listening. It passed.

"You won't give me up?" she cried, seizing his hand.

"I will not," he said, "don't be frightened. Here, I'll take off your wet boots. Mrs Halket's servant will be back directly and she will take care of you. But what has happened? Tell me."

She had little skill in description at any time but she tried to calm herself and to give an account of the black hours she and Maggie had gone through and how she had fled from the ship, panic-stricken and wild with terror of the sea. He could imagine something of it for the morning news sheets had been full of disasters on the coast.

"And you will not let me send word to your husband?" said Aeneas, when she had stopped. "He must be in a terrible state of anxiety. He would surely never wish you to go on when he sees how you have suffered."

"No, no! she cried, hiding her face in her hands, "He doesn't mind—he is angry with me, and you *promised* you'd let no one take me away—"

"But what can we do?" cried Aeneas, desperately, "You'll make yourself ill. As soon as she comes back the maid shall light the fire in your aunt's room and you must go to bed and try to sleep. Your hands are like ice. Tomorrow—"

"Help me to get home," she broke in. "Tomorrow, as soon as I can, I must go. Say you will help me—oh, I pray you to help me. You don't know what dreadful things I've been through to get away! You will—you will—"

Sobbing shook her from head to foot.

"Yes," said Aeneas, slowly, after a pause, "I will."

He was thankful to hear movement in the house, as the maid returned. Never had he been in such a difficult position.

Afterwards when Christina was between the warmed sheets in Mrs Halket's bed, he sat up long by the burnt-out fire. He had promised Christina to get her away and he had learned from her that the *Sirius* would have repairs done before she could sail; he could only hope fervently that Baird might not get on his wife's track that night. Certainly the only thing he could do was to get her home to her father. Poor Christina, with her sodden hair and her lovely hands—he could not understand how she had come to adventure herself out of her calm environment. What had old Lummie Mill been about to let her take a step that a more experienced woman might have shrunk from and walk out of her trim feminine world into the thunderously male one of a ship? He knew nothing about Baird but that he was a first rate seaman and that Mrs Halket had described him as prosperous and popular. As he looked at her, Aeneas told himself that he had never actually been in love with her; yet she attracted him.

Red-eyed and with her draggled garments limp about her, she still appealed to him. He had heard of her engagement with a dim regret—nothing more; and the state of mind described as "feeling out of it" had kept him from going to her wedding, though he would be in Scotland about the time it was to take place.

He lay awake, thinking what he should do in the morning and determining to take her to the earliest train and send her off to her father. He would not go with her for he knew that her return in the company of a young man would set the tongues of her neighbours loose. But he could not fail Christina to whom he had promised protection before she would consent to go to rest and if Baird should appear while she was in the house, his own position might be dreadful.

The railway service of those days gave no great choice of north-going trains but there was one leaving Edinburgh at nine o'clock; and as soon as she was dressed and, compelled by him, had eaten some breakfast, he hurried her away. She had never travelled alone in her life and he commended her to the guard who made himself responsible for her on the strength of what Aeneas gave him.

He watched the train depart with relief. Christina thanked him, her lips quivering. He had held her hand at the carriage door till they started—her pretty hand. She had fled from the ship ungloved, which indecorum distressed her, and the servant had found a pair of gloves belonging to Mrs Halket, gloves whose make and texture shocked

Aeneas. As the train disappeared he turned back to Niven Street; he had let his own house in Gayfield Square and because his stepmother liked him and bore him no malice for its possession she always gave him a bed in his short visits to Edinburgh.

He walked along rather ruefully for his embarrassments were not yet at an end. He felt himself bound to go to Leith and tell the Captain of the *Sirius* of his wife's safety. There must be a hue and cry on the ship by now. He had promised Christina not to give her up to anyone and had been mercifully spared from all difficulty in keeping his word. The security of her father's house would be hers in a few hours and his responsibility was over; but if Baird were ever to hear of the part he had taken he must hear it from no lips but his own. He wished he had not been dragged into it, but what could he have done? Poor little thing! It was dreadful that such a gentle creature should have escaped like a thief through the rough purlieus of Leith docks. She had a dignity, he thought, which had survived her piteous situation that even the drenching and battering of the elements had left intact. Her face, looking trustfully at him from the railway carriage window followed him as, with a resigned sigh, he let himself out of the door of 41 Niven Street and set off for Leith.

Baird, meanwhile, had lost no time; he had raked up a second mate and a couple of journeymen to help the carpenter. The first mate had orders to see that the work went on with all speed and all night. He himself, had not returned till daylight. He was quite sober though he had drunk a good deal and his anger, stirred by his ill-luck, burst out when he heard that Christina was missing. Everyone but the carpenter and the men from the shore was gathered round him as he questioned the crew. Nobody had a word to put forward nor a glimmer of light to throw on how or where Mrs Baird had disappeared till the cook raised his voice.

"Aye," said he, "I mind when I was in the *Mary Ann Macginister* lyin' alangside at Greenock, we had a leddy wi's and i' the nicht she just poupit owre the side o—."

As the torrent with which Baird cut him short abated, the ship's boy was put forward. He had seen a woman on the gangway in the dusk.

"A was settin' down yonder wi' ma piece ahint yon," said he, pointing to the foc'sle door, "an' A saw a wifie gang frae the ship. She didna bide lang. She was awa' in a meenit."

"And why didn't you tell anybody, you damned young limb?"

"A thocht it was Maggie. A didna spier whaur she was gaein'. A thoucht she maybe had a lad waitin' for her." There was a laugh.

36

Baird dismissed the crew and went below. He did not for a moment believe that his wife had gone overboard like the lady in the cook's reminiscences, but he was perturbed by the idea of being delayed by the enquiry that would result should anything untoward have befallen her. Maggie had not left the ship last night, her father said. She had looked at Mrs Baird asleep, but seing that, she had gone to her own bed.

"She was fair done, after sic a nicht," he said.

Baird sent the steward ashore to find out if any of the customary dock labourers had seen anything of Christina and as he ate a hurried breakfast he listened to the hammering overhead and cursed his luck, thinking of how he might be ready to go to sea that night and yet be held back. He did not want the police to get at the matter but, was the steward unsuccessful, he would have to go to them. He certainly had something to complain of.

Eleven o'clock struck as the man came back. He brought word that a stevedore in the Black Horse bar had picked up a tale of a lady wandering near the dock; a sweep had come to the inn asking for some vehicle to take her to Edinburgh. The steward had seen the driver who spoke of a fair young lady and gave the address at which he had set her down.

It was while Baird was taking it down in his pocket book that a young man came along the quay and stopping by the gangway of the *Sirius* called across to know if Captain Baird was on board.

The skipper was in no mood for strangers; the mention of Niven Street had relieved his mind. He had heard that Mrs Halket lived there. The fool of a girl must have forgotten that her aunt was not to return there at once. He looked with impatience at the youth who was stepping on to his deck without so much as a by-your-leave. He was pale and slim and Baird despised his looks as effeminate.

"What's your business?" he asked.

"My name is Halket," replied the other without embarrassment, "and my business is more yours than mine. If we can go where we may speak privately, I can tell it to you."

Baird was not entirely pleased with his companion's imperturbability but he turned without a word and led the way below. They sat down at the table from which the remains of breakfast had not been cleared.

"I thought you must be anxious about Mrs Baird," Halket said, "and I have come to relieve your mind."

He spoke so simply that the skipper's irritation lessened.

"I am obliged to you," he said. "I understand that you know where she is."

37

"I do. She is on her way home."

"Are you sure of that, Mr Halket?"

"I took her to the train myself."

Baird stared. He had never heard of Aeneas.

"Indeed. And what business had you to do it?"

"I am coming to that, Sir, if you will allow me. And I imagine you will say I did right."

"We'll see about that."

"Mrs Baird arrived at my stepmother's door last night. I was never so astonished to see anyone. She was soaked from head to foot and in a terrible state of distress and I brought her in. I could hardly get her calm enough to explain what was wrong. She was nearly mad with terror of the sea and what she had suffered in the storm. The slates had been flying about in Edinburgh and I knew it had been very bad."

"Pshaw!" exclaimed Baird, drumming his fingers on the table.

"She was almost too exhausted to eat and I could only persuade her to let the maidservant put her to bed by promising I would let nobody know where she was. She was in terror lest she should be compelled to go back to sea—so much so that I feared she would make herself ill. But I assured her that no man with the least humanity in him would force her to go back if the sea could bring her to such a state."

"You took a good deal on yourself."

"I did. And I would do it again."

"And so you shipped her back to her father and now you come and tell me about it."

"Exactly," said Aeneas.

Baird did not move but sat considering him. He had the makings of wrath in him for the young man's composure struck him as unsuitable.

"I thought it unfair to you not to let you know that she is safe," said Aeneas. "I have nothing more to say, Sir, and I must be going."

He rose as he spoke. Baird sat still, feeling that Halket should make some apology for what he had done and realising that there was nothing further from the young man's thoughts. What really had kept Baird quiet was the dawning conviction that this meddling fellow had played into his hands. He was now rid of his bad bargain for two voyages.

"I must wish you a good morning," continued Aeneas. "I have business I must go back to."

Baird rose.

"Thanks," he said briskly. "I see you have meant well; and I am obliged to you."

The shock of the amazing apparition of Christina on her father's doorstep was a couple of days old when Baird's letter reached Lummie Mill. The fact that his daughter received none slipped over the bank manager's unperceptive mind like the even flow of water over a stone. The skipper wrote at some length, for he was a man who could use his pen easily; he was sorry, he said, that he had not been able to bring Christina home himself, but duty was duty, as Mr Mill would understand without his telling him, and he had no right to leave his ship on any other business than that of his owner, once the voyage was begun. Christina was quite unfit to endure the sea. The bad weather they had met with had produced a worse effect on her than he had believed possible and he blamed himself because he had not realised how greatly a delicate woman might suffer in the circumstances. He had felt—and here Aeneas' words had come in usefully—that no man with the least humanity would wish her to continue a voyage that could inflict such misery on her. It was very hard on himself, he added but there were times when a man had to think of others, however hard it might be, and he was cheered by the knowledge that his wife had a home in which he knew her to be safe and happy. There followed more in the same suitable strain. There was no possibility of an answer as the *Sirius* was ready to sail as he wrote.

Mill was quite pleased to have his daughter back and after the surprise had worn off everything settled down into the old ways. It was only Mrs Halket who was at all put out. Christina never spoke much and was even more silent. She seemed rather to avoid her aunt and Mrs Halket retired quietly to Niven Street, not wishing to miss her stepson who had been nearer to the centre of upheaval than anybody else.

The town was earnest in its commiseration of its favourite, who had been robbed of his bride in not more than forty-eight hours. Everybody claimed to have foreseen what would happen but as Aeneas Halket kept his own counsel no rumour of her frantic escape reached Christina's neighbours. The terrible weather had upset her health so much that her husband had shirked the responsibility of taking her further and to everyone the flying slates and blown in windows, the toll of wrecks on the coast spoke for themselves.

"Aw! fulishness!" said Ann Wishart. "It was na recht! A young leddy brocht up in a house the like o' Mr Mill's! It was na for the like o' her. But the Captain's tae be hame in a towmont. He'll be tae buy a hoose till her and she'll hae her own kerrage."

Ann was torn between anger that the elements had not respected Mr Mill's daughter and pleasure at being able to vaunt a refinement too great to face them; when Christina's trunks, sent ashore by Baird before sailing, arrived and were unpacked, she insisted on her decking herself in what she would have worn in the antipodes. Maggie had been sent ashore with them, but as her home was in Broughty Ferry no account of her mistress's flight reached the house in the Bow Butts through her. It was as though the whole episode from the day of the *Sirius* first coming and the day when she sailed with Baird and his bride were a dream from which the town had awakened. Lummie Mill, his daughter and the tall hat were in their places in the kirk. None of them had even missed being there, Christina's departure and return having taken place between two Sundays.

It was on one of the calmest and brightest long-lingering summer days when Christina, returned from shopping contentedly in the town, got the news that the *Sirius* had gone down with all hands on that death-trap for Australia-bound ships, King's Island.

VII

The knowledge that she was a widow kept Christina exceedingly thoughtful during the days in which she sat in deep black, behind the drawn-down blinds. Across the world, Baird had been long buried under the seas he had navigated so successfully for more than half of his thirty-six years, but Ann had rigidly closed the eyes of the house till the right time should elapse between a death and a funeral. It would have been an indecency for Christina to go out to order her mourning, so Ann, with Mill's purse at her disposal, swathed her in crape from head to foot. The girl could not see to do her needlework, nor to read had she wished to in the dim light that entered, as she sat in the drawing-room on the spot where she had been proposed to by the dead man. She was awed by her thoughts. The sudden news of his fate had shaken her and brought the startled tears, but she had not really wept though she carried her black-bordered hankerchief in her hand all day. What awed her was the idea of the wrecked ship and she shuddered, remembering that night in the dark cabin with Maggie and the intolerable ringing of the ship's bell as they were flung about in the jaws of the seas. She was glad to think Maggie was safe and not drowned with the others. Had it been like that night—the hour when they were lost? Perhaps they had gone down to the ringing of that bell and its voice had clanged on till the waters swallowed them. She had not the imagination that will picture distant events in an ordinary way but she had never been able to look back on her short voyage without hearing its crying tongue. Her eyes went over the familiar furniture surrounding her father's footstool to his place on the hearth; the stiff portrait of him as a young man over the mantelpiece, and she was grateful for their reassuring sameness. She was at home— back with them—and yet she was that definite thing, a widow. She felt even more conscious of taking her place in life than when she had stood up in this room to be married. The thought of Baird drowning came upon her and she sobbed, not from grief but from the horror of his end. Perhaps the same end had been near that night when the bell was ringing.

She got up and went down to the kitchen where she could be near Ann and away from the dim light. Ann's kingdom looked on the back of the house and the blinds would be up there. She was a widow. She would have to do as widows did and she had never heard of a new made widow sitting in the kitchen. She paused. Perhaps she ought not to do it but she could not help thinking of the bell when she was alone. She went dwn stairs in her rustling silk and crape. Ann was stirring something on the fire and looked up.

"Eh, Mistress Baird, this is no place for you!" she cried. "Dinna sit there by the window! Maybe the flesher's laddie'll gae by wi the meat an' it would be an awfae thing if he saw ye there i' the noo! Bide you aside the door whaur ye can win oot easy."

"It's so dark upstairs, Ann, and I've nothing to do. Couldn't I do something to help you?"

"Na, na, ye mauna. Did anybody ever hear the like! Just compose yersel', Mistress Baird."

"But I am not *very* unhappy, Ann."

"Whisht! Whisht! ye dinna ken what ye're sayin'."

"But it's true. Oh, I'm so thankful I was not drowned—I'm so thankful to be home."

"Ye'll dae better yet," rejoined Ann "Ye'll be gettin' a grand hoose o' yer ain. Ye'll be weel left, I'll warrant. Aye, we'll be seein' ye estaiblished."

Christina had given no thought to the future. Some little time must elapse before her husband's business affairs could be settled and her prospects of money made clear; she sat wishing Ann would not force her up against details she was unprepared to face. She was at home and that was all that mattered.

"I don't know anything about that. I am quite happy here."

"Maybe," said Ann. "Ye'll hae tae be estaiblished, for a' that."

41

The more Ann struck forward to the future, the more Christina drew back to the past. Only now, when she had been cut free from the life in which she had entangled herself, like some timid creature strayed into a gamekeeper's snare, could she venture to look behind her; and she liked doing it because it made the darkened house seem light by contrast.

"It is dreadful to be on a ship," she said. "I was so frightened. The light went out in the night and there was only Maggie, the girl, beside me."

Ann was cooking. "And whaur was the Captain?" she enquired, over her shoulder.

"I didn't see him at all in the storm."

In grim silence, Ann turned around.

"He should hae ken't better," she said at last.

"He was too busy. He had no time."

"He should na hae left ye."

"But he had to mind the ship, Ann."

"*He should na hae left ye*," said Ann, firmly.

"Ann, you don't understand."

But Ann had turned back to her fire again.

"I understand what's due till a young leddy like you," she replied in a repressed voice. "Dinna haver tae me—and you a bride! Ye mauna speak ill o' deid folk, but lord! A wouldna hae believed it! and you Miss Mill! But ye'll dae better yet; aye, will ye!"

Christina sat twisting her black-bordered handkerchief. She wondered which was the worst, the kitchen or the lugubrious drawing-room, as the step of the butcher's lad fell on the flagged court outside.

"Awa' wi ye, Mistress Baird!" cried Ann. Christina fled.

Ann threw open the back door.

"It's a sad hoose we hae here," she said, as she received the meat he brought.

"It will be," replied he.

"But she's bearin' up."

The boy was hardly thirteen and unused to dealing single-handed with solemn topics, so he said nothing.

"Aw the *expense*!" exclaimed Ann. "Ye wouldna believe what the gentry has tae tak' frae their pocket when there's a death!"

He was bewildered. The costly pomps of funerals was all he could think of.

"Was he washed up?" he asked, almost in a whisper.

"Ye haverin' trash!" cried Ann.

But he was a practical child.

"Ye canna hae a bur'al wantin', the corp," he observed doggedly.

"Div' ye think there's nae mair tae't nor that? Corp or nae corp, A tell ye Mistress Baird's blacks' had tae be the best. Haud awa' wi ye, now—what div the like o' you ken aboot the gentry? See now, here's the basket."

She pushed him off. She was satisfied, in spite of her contempt, for she hoped he would repeat every word she had said to him to his mother.

It was a sad surprise to her when Baird's money affairs were wound up and Christina's prospects made known; she had built on the assumption that he would come back a rich man from this voyage or another. But he would never come back from any voyage and his widow had no more than a modest income and asked no better than to live with her father in the house in the Bow Butts; the only difference that Ann could see in her importance was the matronly title on her few letters and the billowing majesty of her 'blacks'. And even the latter would be modified in time.

Ann's opinion of Baird was modifying too. He had had no right to presume to Christina's hand and she began to obliterate his memory in a sea of silence as deep as the sea that lay upon his body. His widow was silent too and when the first anniversary of her wedding passed and that of her widowhood followed, it was marked by a faint abatement in the rigour of her mourning. The captain's masterful shadow had left the house; there were none of his small possessions about nor letters to destroy, for the former had been lost with him and the latter, owing to his presence in the town during the whole of his courtship, had no existence.

Before the last trace of her weeds had disappeared Christina sat on a morning of early Autumn under one of the trees by the house reading a letter the post had just brought her. Its torn wrapper lay on the ground at her feet. She had changed a little in the two years since her marriage for her face had lost a trifle of its youth and gained something in confidence. She was thirty and the fact gave her the mild astonishment that comes to most people on starting a new decade.

She knew the writing that lay on her knee.

My dear Mrs Baird [Aeneas Halket wrote],

                       I have long intended to write to you and an event has occurred that has taken away my last hesitation in doing so. I have been made a partner in my business and with this good fortune at my back, I feel I have a better

43

right to tell you what I have had in my heart for some time. You may not know—how should you—that you have always held a particular place in my mind. In the couple of years before your marriage I had almost told you of those feelings of regard but my not having a definite home to offer you kept me silent. I was just beginning to see my way when I heard of your approaching marriage, and almost before I could adjust my mind to the misfortune of having delayed too long, you arrived at my stepmother's house on the memorable evening when I had the chance of serving you in your difficulty. When I heard you were a widow, respect for custom kept me again silent during the term of your deeper mourning. But it is two years since the wreck of the *Sirius* and I think I may be justified in declaring myself. If you will be my wife I will try to make you happy. I am in a position to give you a home in which I hope you will have everything to which you are accustomed as well as a husband who will love you sincerely. I trust you will give me the answer I hope for. . . .

As she laid the letter down just below Aeneas Halket's signature she saw a pencilled line. "I like to think that this paper will be held in your beautiful hands."

It was not exactly an ardent letter but its steady kindness was perhaps the thing to commend it most to her and the few words at the end gave her a shy pleasure. She held out her hands with her luckless wedding ring on one of them and examined them. She was glad Aeneas admired them still. She got up and went in, leaving the envelope lying by her chair.

Up in her room, she put the letter in her workbox and turned the key; then she went to a drawer and took out the picture of the modish St Cecilia and set it in its old place on the mantelpiece, considering it. It had almost been forgotten but she liked it and its presence there committed her to nothing, she told herself. The question of marriage could be deferred for a short time. He could not expect her to make up her mind without consideration.

That evening Ann Wishart went out to fetch in Christina's chair and picking up the envelope, saw the French script. She had often seen that writing on letters to Mrs Halket and she knew very well whence it came.

There was only one post daily yet Christina who had been looking over house linen with Ann, that afternoon, had not said a word about what was probably lying in her pocket all the time. Ann drew down her mouth and reflected that marriage made people "very close".

44

It was some time before the hoped opportunity came. Christina was in her bedroom when Ann knocked and, going up to her with a wooden face, held out the envelope.

"Ye left that i' the garden, Mistress Baird. I've been tae gie't ye this while. Maister Halket'll be weel?"

"Oh yes. He has been made partner in his business. He knew we should be pleased to hear that. He will be quite rich," added Christina, leaving the room lest she should be further questioned.

It was all but a fortnight before she could make up her mind to answer Aeneas; she liked the idea of his affection, but though the chain of habit that bound her so long had been violently cut it had not been severed long enough to prevent the ends from joining anew. She was still luxuriating in the unruffled peace to which she had been miraculously restored and Aeneas' constancy was like some pleasant book in the shelf whose back recalls its contents without the trouble of opening it. The town was beginning to forget she had ever been away.

She had written to Aeneas, asking for time to consider. Lummie remained ignorant for she was loth to utter a word that seem to crystallize what she hoped at present to keep vague. Meantime in Ann's mind, Aeneas' star was rising.

"Aye, she'll hae tae be estaiblished," she would say to herself as she watched the clicking jack turn in front of the bars with its load of meat. The great weights like millstones hung at the corner of the kitchen and the ropes that worked them ran like a narrow frieze round the walls. She imagined Christina's kitchen, her chandeliered dining-room and the noble joints that would travel from one to the other to steam on a rich man's table at the head of which Christina would preside; the green venetian blinds behind the silk-clad figure were almost visible to her gaze and the carriage drive outside them. She would stand still contemplating her vision with the eye of faith.

Christina had not told Aeneas whether she required a week or a month or a year for consideration. But some day the letters would have to be answered and the simpering face of St Cecilia would remind her of it. And there was not a day when Ann did not set her personal view of her duty before her; she had long ago guessed the contents of Aeneas' letter.

"Ye'll see," she said to Christina, "that Maister Mill'll no be left langer than ony other body. He just wants a year o' saxty-four. Him and ma brither James is ages. Saxty-three, the pair o' them. Ye're young yet but ye'll hae tae see and be estaiblished afore ye're left yer lane. It's no

45

muckle the Captain did for ye—he was ane o' they folk that doesna keep what they get. Mind you, A'm no sayin' ye hae the need tae better yersel for ye'll be weel left when Maister Mill's awa'; but I'd like fine tae see ye in yer carriage. And a man's a man; gin I'd had a lad like Halket seekin' me I'd no hae been sic a fule as let him gang. No me."

"Ann, why did you never marry?" asked Christina, suddenly. "Did you ever—like anyone?"

"Aye, did I."

"But are you sorry? Do you mind now?" continued Christina stupidly.

"Am I mindin'?" cried Ann, turning on her, "Div ye think that there's onybody pleased that has naethin' o' their ain? Are ye thinkin' it's a grand thing tae gang intae the kirk-yard and niver hae gotten a man or a wean?"

At sight of her quivering face a measure of comprehension came to Christina—a small measure.

"I'm so sorry, Ann," she exclaimed, kindly, standing still and staring. "But you've got me, you know," she added after a moment.

For reply, the other flung from her, banging the door. She had looked at her as if she hated her.

Christina had never known her as anything but masterful, certain, invulnerable; a mainstay. The young widow was not naturally selfish but she had not been forced by life to think much of anyone but herself. Her father, wrapped up like a packet in the padding of his own small affairs, was independent of her sympathies; her aunt had no need of them. Though she was truly grieved to find that Ann had lacked anything to make her happy, Christina's feeling was one of absolute astonishment.

There seemed to be so much round her that she had never imagined. She began to guess how much mistaken it is possible to be in things taken for granted. Would she ever feel as Ann—the unfailing Ann—felt? She remained planted on the spot, wondering.

There was nothing, next day, to remind her of the depths opened before her, yesterday. Ann was as decided and trenchant as ever, but Christina felt shaken. In the scheme of things that could so unnerve Ann what chance of security was there for herself? All at once the coming years looked forlorn. Might she have to go through an unknown dimness crowded with unrevealed experiences lying in wait for her? Why should she be at the mercy of chances and changes when those she knew— placid neighbours and accepted acquaintances—seemed to have nothing to disturb their equanimity? In her innocent egotism she thought of herself as the sole sufferer from the hazards of what should be stable things—not exactly the sole sufferer, perhaps, but the one who would feel them most. It was through these troubled pools of thought that there swam up the thought that Aeneas Halket had been her shield in the extremity of her need, had listened to her and stood between her and her terror. She did not want to marry anybody but she trusted Aeneas, though she was too unsophisticated to gauge the position he had faced on her account. Men will face artillery, bulls, epidemics, the duties of steeplejacks, savages and fire—all the licensed dangers that inhabit this tormented earth—but not one in a hundred will stand up to the risk of ridicule or misconstruction where there is the shadow of a petticoat in the matter. It was part of Aeneas' misfortune that Christina was the last woman alive who would understand the cold-blooded courage of what he had done. She was grateful to him but not more so than if she had slipped and hurt herself in the street and he had given her his arm home.

Before long another letter came.

Dear Christina,

I am not trying to press you for an answer though I am hoping for one every day. It is on a matter of business that I have to write now. The lease of my house in Gayfield Square will run out at the term and the tenant is asking me to renew it. I should be willing to do so, had I not another prospect at heart. I am hoping to require it for myself and to see you mistress of it. As I have said, I am not trying to hurry you and you will admit that I am patient, but I cannot keep my tenant waiting. It is not fair to him. I could not live in that house alone. It is too large for a single man and there is no use in letting it stand empty. I am waiting for you to tell me what I should do. There is no need for me to repeat what I said in my last letter, for it all stands the same. I shall hope for your answer soon. . . .

Christina looked up from her reading. She was almost glad that something tangible and important like the lease of a house had sprung up to make her decision necessary. Vacillation is one of the most painful things in the world and yet there are some people that can never have enough of it and she was beginning to suffer a mental giddiness from its see-saw. She knew that Ann had no hesitations on the subject; and that now she was indisputably at the turning-point, brought there by the lease, she was almost more afraid to speak to her father. To him she had never mentioned the subject of the future because its discussion had always been shut off behind the same curtain of mysterious delicacy that shrouded any serious allusion to love, religion or money; but this was a reality—a lease!

"Papa," she began, "Mr Halket has written me a letter—" she stopped; it was not easy.

"It'll be a proposal!" he exclaimed with a giggle.

"But it is about his house," she said, growing confused.

"He wants to know if he should let it—I mean, he will let it if I do not marry him. What shall I do?"

"What do you mean?" said he, bewildered too. "I don't understand."

"He wants me to marry him and live in the house—I don't know—"

Lummie slapped his leg and crowed, as if he had found out a conjuring trick.

"I knew it was an offer!" he cried.

"But had I better say 'yes', Papa?"

"Why not, my dear? He's a nice lad. I always liked Aeneas."

"I really don't know what is best."

"Take him, my dear, of course. I could believe you'll do better this time." He pursed his lips with elaborate wisdom and repeated his words.

"You'll likely be better suited this time."

She would have spoken again but he was looking with a sort of prim joviality into space.

"There'll be another wedding breakfast!" he cried.

She awoke next morning to the necessity of writing her letter. She had delayed too long and her conscience smote her. Her father had been acquiescent though he seemed to give his consideration more to the details of the wedding than to the desirability of its taking place; and when she had parted from him last night, the engagement was understood to be settled. She now sat at the little walnut writing table in the drawing room; her handwriting was rather pretty and she expressed herself better on paper than in speaking. When the letter was addressed she put on her hat with its long feather that swept over the brim just behind her ear for she meant to carry it to the post office and then to return to tell Ann what she had done.

In the September sunshine, an attractive and decorous figure in her billowing lavender-coloured skirt and drooping plume, she had some grace of movement and as she passed along the stony greyness of the street a couple of passers-by looked after her and wondered whether Captain Baird's widow would marry again.

The remembrance came to her of another walk through grey streets; but then, they had been dark and soaking and she was lost and terrified as she fled from that nightmare in which the bell's desolate clanging had rung crazily out among the thrashing seas. She rejoiced that Aeneas was no longer employed in France and that she need never set foot in a ship again.

This letter of acceptance that she carried must be the beginning of a far safer venture than the last one and she was doing a wise thing for herself and an apparently satisfactory one to her relations. Mrs Halket had been away in England for some weeks but she would be pleased when she heard the news. Christina wished that her aunt were with her now, because, though she was convinced of the wisdom of her action, she would have liked someone beside Ann Wishart to uphold her definitely. But that was a foolish feeling, no doubt.

She walked on in her voluminous folds of lavender. The post office was a small place tucked away below the town hall, a stone's throw from the steeple under whose shadow she had first met Baird.

The long High Street was rather hazy at its further end in the mistiness of light that comes to the East Coast before the full poignancy of autumn. A good many figures were moving about because it was market day, but the place was not thronged, the main thoroughfare being so spacious.

Some way off on the pavement Lummie Mill was coming towards her and she could see the movement of his hat among the heads of the people. She was at the entrance to the post office, just about to cross the threshold, when, as she paused with her hand on the door, the vision of the well-known shape that had always been one with her father's existence and inseparable from him, brought, in a staggering rush to her heart, an assaulting realisation of the surroundings that had been her life and without which she could not live; childhood, her placid existence, her home; the chain of Sundays stretching back into vacancy on which she had sat in the pew under the gallery; that background into which her soul, as well as her body, had fitted so smoothly and safely. In the very jaws of her decision, the sight of the tall hat intensified her consciousness of these things a thousand fold. Here had been security, shelter, all that was best. And they were about to go from her by her own act.

She turned quickly and in a few minutes had let herself in at the door of the house in the Bow Butts.

Like a thief she hurried noiselessly upstairs and tore up her letter, thrusing its fragments into the drawing-room fire.

➤ The Fifty-Eight Wild Swans ➤

The only person who had any control over old Jimmy Strachan was Maria Mitchell, his niece, who lived in the cottage adjoining his own. He was seventy-six, and when he retired from work, much crippled by rheumatism and with a bad heart, he had gone into this particular dwelling so that Maria, a widow woman, would be able to do his cooking. He was a bachelor who had no hobbies, despised gardening, and read nothing but the newspaper, which he could do without spectacles, for his sight was wonderful. His mouth was twisted with years of ill temper and his powerful hands with rheumatism; this had now become worse, and made walking a dreadful exertion, very bad for his heart. He was not without pleasures, because he was greedy, and Maria was a splendid cook. She saw to it that he was comfortable, for she was a hard, confident woman and liked doing things thoroughly, tall and stout, with the black, thick watchful eye of a gander. Strachan's fits of temper produced no more effect upon Maria than if they had taken place in the moon, instead of next door; and it was not in his power to do anything to annoy her but abuse the food she set before him, which he was far too wise to do. He was comfortably off, with his savings and his old-age pension. He had all he wanted and could keep himself handsomely in tobacco.

In good weather Strachan would sit in his garden, for while he despised the place as an ornament, he liked it as a point from which he could talk to passers-by when he was in the humour for it, though they were little inclined to loiter for the pleasure of his company. It was a fairly frequented road down which an occasional motor car sped or a motor cyclist rushed by to disappear between the hedges like an escaping goblin. His underhung jaw and startling white eyebrows made children uncomfortable, and some of them were afraid when they saw him looking out with his pipe between the teeth. Alister MacHugh, an inquisitive, solemn, cautious child of twelve who lived farther up the road, was not afraid, because he reasoned very sensibly that, Strachan being almost crippled, could not reach him if he wanted to, and that hard words, if they come over a thorn hedge, lose much of their menace. He liked staring at the old man and was attracted in the same way that some people are attracted by such horrors as they can contemplate in safety.

An acquaintance had begun between these two which approached toleration, though it went no further. Strachan disliked the bold children, who were often rude, but the timid ones, who would run by looking back at him as if he were a buffalo in a cage, were those he could least endure, perhaps because the beast-in-the-cage idea came home to him too much; for he had been a very active man and the stultified and superintended comfort in which Maria kept him grated on some fierce thing in him, though he would have resented its absence.

The acquaintance had begun one day when Alister passed and came to a standstill before Strachan's house. The old man hobbled as far as the garden gate and leaned upon its rail, smoking. The boy was used to seeing the upper part of him, but the lower half had always been concealed by the hedge, and he was now interested in the revelation of the whole through the bars. It was a chance not to be missed. His eyes were fixed on the thick, cramped figure which scowled with lowered head at the leggy one in the road. Neither spoke, but a wordless growl came over the gate. Many another brat would have run, but Alister MacHugh's ponderous interest and plain good sense kept him still.

Presently there was not a growl, but a shout, and in its accomplishment Strachan's pipe fell and, striking the rail, rebounded on to the road. It was a good briar pipe and was none the worse, but it lay well out of reach of the stick. In his heart he was dismayed, because of the hostility taken for granted between himself and the young. One kind of child would make off with the pipe and hide it, and the other kind would not approach him with it.

But Alister MacHugh belonged to neither sort. When a thing falls you pick it up, if only to see what it feels like to have it in your hand. Strachan was so much astounded to get his treasure returned that he did not so much as say thank you; in fact, he was rather angry at losing a fraction of his general grievance against the youth of his parish. Alister MacHugh went on his way wrapped in the impersonal placidity which attended him. Strachan watched him out of sight, and it dawned on his cross-grained mind that here was a being curiously unlike anyone else.

The infinitesimal tinge of approval which the episode left with the old man had been imperilled by their next meeting.

"Dinna cowp yer pipe," Alister had said, pausing as he passed. Strachan drew in his breath and his brows lowered. But there was no shade of impudence in the words, merely an obvious plainness of thought, and the occasion sailed by safely, like a leaf on a running stream that has been almost side-tracked by a rock.

Nobody who knew Strachan had the faintest notion that any gleam of romance had ever illuminated his mind. He had never been known to look at a woman nor listen to a song nor go to any place of entertainment, but the public house, and there he drank little and talked less; he had never shown a preference for anybody. But the neighbours did not know everything about him. He had come from another part of Scotland, a lad of nineteen, and nobody had troubled to ask how he had spent his earlier life; he slipped into farm work like other people, and his companions were unaware that he had been in the employ of a wild-fowler somewhere on the border.

Those had been the halcyon days of Strachan's life, and their remembrance stayed with him; the flighting duck; the skein of wild geese lacing the skies in rhythmic loops of pulsating wings; the sound of their remote voices; the flap of a heron beating up out of the rushes to disappear with the long curve of his neck laid back till his breast-bone looked like the prow of a Viking ship against the atmosphere. At that time his own "thrawnness" had obscured from him the knowledge of how happy he was. Now he admitted to himself his crass unawareness of his luck. A gull flying inland or the cry of any large bird would stir him, no matter what he was doing. He spoke of these things to nobody.

Less than a mile from his cottage there was a sheet of water lying solitary in a stretch of flat land. A traveller, knowing where to look for it, might, from the road, see its gleam through the alders beyond the fields. On its northern side the ground sloped gently to a farm whose steading was the only thing to suggest human occupation, and, beyond this, lay the Grampians on the horizon. On the western end of the water was a narrow belt of green shore on the confines of which stood high fir woods. Though the place was so near cultivation, it had an aloofness that seemed to remove it miles away; lying idly on its eastern side and looking across, you might expect to see some tall befeathered Indian step out from between the fir-stems and launch his noiseless canoe. There were duck there and coot, and once or twice in living memory a wild swan or two had come down from the Findhorn and made a transitory sojourn in the quiet spot.

The cold set in early that year; by the beginning of November the winds were bitter and there was a good deal of rain. The east coast was dark with stormy twilights; the late leaves came whirling to the ground to be chased and harried to death in damp corners. Tattie-lifting was over and Alister MacHugh, who had been assisting at it, was back at school again when suddenly the wind went into the north and the sopping earth began to harden. The nights were black, for the moon had just gone out of her last quarter, but they were still. It was between one and two in the morning when Jimmy Strachan, lying wakeful, heard a sound that made him drag himself painfully up in bed. He sat with clenched hands pressed against his chest and eyes turned towards the window. Like most of his kind, he slept with it shut, and though the curtain was not drawn, there was no gleam of starlight to reveal its sunken square. His heart beat against his ribs, but he held his breath. Through the dead stillness came the long cry of the whooper swan.

Again—again. From the direction of that sleeping water beyond the fields the voices flowed out of the air. He rose, hobbling and groping, till his hand was on the matchbox. As he lit the candle and the flame caught, the cry rang out afresh. He pressed his face to the window pane, but he could not so much as see where the garden hedge ended and the sky began, and after shivering a few minutes he went back to bed, pinching out the flame with his broad fingers. Though he drew his blankets close, the moisture broke out on his forehead at the thought that, even should morning find the stranger birds lying like anchored ships not a mile away, he would not be able to see them. His disabilities leaned over him and knocked upon his heart, stifling his breath. The dark hours were bitter to him till he slept.

When he awoke the candle was lit again and Maria, who had come in from next door with her head muffled in a shawl, was raking the ash from the fire. The cup of tea she had brought steamed beside him and the clock-hands pointed to seven.

"Tak' yer tea when it's het," she said.

He did not move.

"Tak' yer tea, I tell ye—what ails ye? Are ye no weel?"

He sat up and took a tentative sip, noisy and prolonged.

"I'm weel eneuch. Did ye no hear onything i' the nicht?"

"Was ye cryin' on me?"

He made a contemptuous sound.

"There'll be swans upo' the water out yonder," he said. "I heard the skellach (cry) o' them."

"Maybe," she said.

"An' there'll be mair nor ane."

"Haste-ye noo. I'm needin' the cup."

"But ye did no hear them?" he persisted, sticking out his under lip.

"Dod! What wad I dae list'nin' on the like o' yon?"

"I heard them," said he, doggedly.

"Tuts! Ye heard the swine at the back o' the hoose."

"A *swine*?" he exclaimed, with wrath.

But she had gone out. He dragged himself out of bed. There was nothing to be got from Maria and he must find some better source of news.

As soon as he had dressed he went out, in spite of the cold, and established himself in the garden. It was Monday; and on Mondays the farmer north of the water sent his grieve to the town. Every Monday he passed on his way to the station. The old man went to the gate as he saw the familiar figure approach.

"Ony news?" he asked.

"Na, fegs!" said the other. "Naethin' tae dae onybody ony guid. But they tell me the water out yonder's just fair fu' o' birds. Swans, they say. Auld Tibbie Mowatt that bides oot yon way was sayin' she couldna get sleepit the streen for their noise—dirty brutes. Fufty-aicht o' them."

"Maybe they're awa' by this," said Strachan, his words almost sticking in his throat.

"I dinna think it. They're sittin' as canny as sheep intill a field, Tibbie said."

Strachan was speechless. Fifty-eight! he felt as if he were suffocating. He knew that, impossible though it must be for him to see them, a part of him could not give up the hope. He went into the house and sat down and the whole anguish of his helplessness came over him. The desire of his eyes was so near, and yet he could never see it. Fifty-eight! He put his hand over his surly face. His lids were wet.

Then began a very torment of unrest. He tried to read his newspaper, but he could take in nothing. He left it and went out again to see whether anyone was coming by who could tell him more of the sight that would be so much to him, so little to anyone else. And all the time he knew that, were he to talk of it to the whole parish, he would be brought no nearer to what he longed for, ached for. He was like a little schoolboy, piteous over some promised delight refused at the last moment.

The day went heavily by, and at night he turned his face to the wall and tried to forget those white phantoms that came between him and his rest. But again he awoke in the stillness and heard the voices calling across the darkened fields.

Next day the baker's van stopped at Maria's door. He could hear the driver telling her of the swans. He had seen them from that bit of his road from which the water was visible.

"Ye should awa' an' see them," said he as he handed out her two loaves.

"Heuch!" she cried, snorting, "muckle time I hae for rinnin' after birds!"

The driver looked round and saw Strachan in his garden.

"Aweel," said he, with eyes sociably including the old man in the converstion, "there's mony wad like fine tae get a sicht o' them, nae doot."

"Fine, fine wad I like it!" burst out Strachan, his hide of surliness penetrated by the mere shadow of a sympathetic outlook, "an' maybe, gin I could get a ride—"

Maria's gander eye was upon him.

"Ye needna think tae try that," she exclaimed, "you that canna sae muckle as win tae the kirk!"

"Wha askit ye?" shouted Strachan, losing his temper, "I wasna speakin' tae ye—haud yer wisht, ye bizzar!"

"Ye needna seek tae win out o' this, gin *I'm* here," she said, as she went in with her loaves.

The van drove on and Strachan, with a bursting heart, made for his fireside.

He sat down, breathing hard from exertion and wrath and humiliation, and the tears, whose compelling rush age and the sense of his helplessness alone could force from his stubborn soul, welled up and ran down his nose, dropping on the back of Maria's cat, which sometimes came in to enjoy a quiet not always available at home. He knew by experience that Maria always attained her objects somehow.

Time went by; the clock struck more than once and he did not move; he had often heard it said that there is a way out of everything, if you can only find it, and he stared at the fire as though, by glaring long enough, he might see in its depths some path of relief in his passionate need. When he rose at last a step on the road made him look out. Beyond the bars of the garden gate he saw Alister MacHugh returning from school to his dinner. A great light entered into his mind.

When his own meal was brought in he could hardly touch it. He had fetched a shilling from the cupboard and was squeezing it in his hand as Alister came back on his return journey, and the boy was surprised to see him in his doorway, beckoning him in with wordless signs. He stood still, considering whether he should respond, but reflecting that he had never seen the inside of Strachan's dwelling, he opened the gate. At the threshold he was haled in.

55

As he left, ten minutes later, Strachan shook him by the arm.

"Ye'll no tell onybody what ye're tae dae," he said, gripping him fiercely.

"Dinna roog me. I ken fine."

"And ye'll no let on tae the dominie," continued Strachan, shaking him. "Na. He's an auld gowk."

When the boy got home that evening he stowed his coin away in some corner known to himself. He had left Strachan's door with the prospect of another shilling if he carried out the plan that the old man had unfolded. There were some risks attending it and a great deal of secrecy: the former did not seem to him so very startling (as he did not know Maria), and the latter he loved.

Strachan was going to try to reach his goal on his own feet and he had chosen Alister as an accomplice for excellent reasons. The scheme was so wild that only a child would consent to take part in it, and he also knew in an undefined way that Alister's qualities were not all childish ones. Saturday was the school holiday and Maria was going to Arbroath for the day, and these coinciding events would make the scheme possible; but he hated the delay, fearing that the swans should take flight before the week was out. It was two years since he had been more than a stone's throw from home for the mere crossing of his garden was an effort; it took so much force to move his bent body and stiff joints. He had long made up his mind, with what was more like callousness than resignation, to the restraints of age and fate, but now his callousness had broken down. He was going to see the wild swans, cost what it might, if only Maria did not hear of it and terrorise Alister into withholding his help. Then, indeed, he would be undone.

It was the first part of the journey that made him anxious. Once across the road and into the stubble field opposite, he might be unseen by any officious neighbour. At the farther side of it there was a gate into the green loaning choked with broom, and along this he would reach a strip of wood that ended on the waste ground by the water. He neither cared nor considered how he was to get back. He could see no further than the swans. All the week he watched the heavens, dreading that, in their wrath with his madness, they might pour with sufficient malice to keep Maria at home.

But Saturday dawned, one of the strangest and most beautiful days that had befallen this autumn. The week had ended as though bewitched. Frost had set in and, with it, a clear whiteness and stillness in which all nature seemed to hold its breath. The tall trees by the loan stood drawn up like an array waiting motionless for some word of awe that was to come through the spellbound air. The atmosphere was steely, ecstatic; the sun was faint in it. The larger lines of the landscape were sharp and full of meaning, like divine truths. You might feel that your faculties were interchangeable—that you saw with your mind, understood with your eyes; or, rather, that you needed no faculties, because everything was resolved into its essence.

Maria brought his food for the day and departed. She expected to be home by three. Alister, conveniently ambushed, watched her round the turn of the road before betaking himself to Strachan's cottage. The old man was sitting gripping the arm of his chair; the moment was come, and his hand shook as he signed to the boy to fetch his warm coat from the peg.

The door key lay in his pocket as they crossed the garden painfully, but a kind of false strength had come to him and his spirits rose. The highway was clear, and Alister got him across it and between the gaping gateposts into the field. They proceded slowly, neither speaking, for both had need of breath as they struggled along. Every ridge hardened by the frost, every declivity was a jar to the old man, but his lips were set, and with his arm laid on Alister's immature shoulder, he pushed doggedly forward. The boy felt his weight so much that he had to revive his courage with the thought of the shilling in Strachan's pocket, which would be transferred to his own when they reached the waterside. Four times in their crawling progress through the stubble they stopped to rest; Strachan's pale face and deep breaths told of the torture of his efforts. Once he almost fell. They reached the loan, and behind an ambuscade of broom halted so that he could lean against a stake. Alister's shoulder was numb and his legs felt as if they were misfits. The ditches beside them were full of ice. Their breath rose in hot vapour.

In a little while they began their *via dolorosa* again.

"I should hae gotten a drappie whuskey wi' me," said Strachan, stopping and panting when they had gone a few yards; "sic a dawmed fule I was no tae tak' ma boattle alang wi's."

The MacHughs were a teetotal family.

"It's pushon (poison)," said Alister, solemnly.

Strachan's ready anger flamed up, but he dared not give vent to it. It would take more energy than he could spare to say what he thought, but he ground his arm viciously down on Alister's collar bone. The boy wriggled.

"I'm no for gangin' on," he exclaimed, wavering.

"Twa shillin's—twa—," gasped Strachan.

They moved forward.

All things come to an end at last, and they were approaching the wood. It was terrible ground for such as Strachan to travel. Tussocks, coming against his stumbling feet, were like lumps of cement and the frozen ruts like stone coping; as the sides of his boots grated on them shocks of fire ran up his knee joints. In spite of the cold, sweat stood upon his forehead. He was past recking of anything but his goal and the conflict he waged against weakness and suffering. In the beech wood giddiness attacked him and he swayed against the boy.

"I canna haud ye up," whimpered Alister.

"Twa shillin's—twa shillin's," groaned Strachan between his teeth.

He leaned against a young tree and clung with convulsive hands to its lower boughs, while the earth seemed to rock and gravitation to be at an end. Through his reeling senses a swan's cry floated, half submerged, as sea tangle on Atlantic waves.

"They're no awa'," he whispered when he came out of the grip of the disintegrating terror.

Slowly they added another hundred yards to the tale of their grievous progress; their task was growing short and the path was near its turn into the open. Horizontal gleams beyond the stems told of the water.

The sun was beginning to dominate the upper air as they set foot on the boggy turf, now firm with frost. Beside them a row of thin rowans displayed the yellowing leaves on their shiny dark branches; the berries had long gone down the throat of the greedy missel thrush. Here the labouring figures stopped and Strachan lifted his eyes.

They were there—the creatures of his desire, of his troubled sleep, his bitter wakings, his long thoughts. He put up the ancient field glass that had hung for years behind his door and saw the snowy line laid along the ice, showing here and there a ripple of movement. Now that he had accomplished his end he was hardly able to bear it.

"They're owre many tae coont," he said, thickly; "coont you, laddie."

He held out the glass.

"Whaur's ma boab?" said Alister MacHugh.

"Coont you and ye'll get it. Can ye see?"

"Aye, div I, Ane, twa—began Alister.

When he he had passed fifty Strachan grew impatient and took the glass away. "Here's tae ye," he said. But his hand trembled so that the shilling fell at their feet. Alister picked it up.

"It was tae be twa."

58

But Strachan's pockets were empty. He had forgotten when he made his lavish promises, that he had only one coin. His truculence seemed to have left him.

"I haena got anither," he replied, rather shakily, "But ye'll get it when we win hame."

The boy contemplated him with still disapproval. He did not doubt the words, but he felt defrauded.

"A'm tae bide a bit," said the other. "Give me a haund till I sit doon."

When this had been done, Strachan devoured the spectacle before him with sunken yet piercing eyes. Alister went off towards the wood, dragging his feet; his shoulder was stiff and he dragged them in protest as boys will. The deferred shilling rankled and the less satisfactory aspects of the adventure took more importance in his mind. The day had passed noon. He began to think about his dinner, less because he was hungry than because his absence would have to be accounted for, and he guessed that, should any harm come to Strachan, and he were known to have abetted his exploit, he might get into trouble. He loitered, irresolute. Should he stay here, awaiting Strachan's pleasure or should he run home, escape privily after dinner and come back to finish his task? The absence of the second shilling turned the scale. He departed quickly.

Strachan's head began to clear and his senses to take in the sight before him. A more indifferent beholder than the one who now looked on it might well be overpowered by its wonder. It was like a vision isolated from the clamourous earth, a glory cast from something remote and set, for a space, within the cognisance of men. The air was as still as though time had stopped; but carried over the frozen water came that indefinable stir which hardly amounts to a sound, that muffled vibration emanating from collective creatures. Over the sharp clarity of ice, turned to metallic indigo with the sun's strengthening, it travelled like a breath. Beyond, across the polished surface, the wall of firwood rose in dense and sombre mass, its foot lost in the grey blueness of mist that had not yet withdrawn from the farther shore. The crowded line of swans stretched in a thick bar against it, and now from one part of the line, now from another, a white, sinuous neck would raise itself and cut into the blur of tree-stems and vapour.

Strachan gazed on; weary with holding the glass, he leaned back against a rowan. His sight was still so keen that not a movement of that snow-coloured company was lost on him, not the uplifting of a curved neck, not the extended arch of a shifting wing. The dark blue ice under

the birds flung up their white beauty against the austere mystery of the woods. He had never beheld the like, not in his young days, not in the careless times when he had been free to go about in the strength of his powerful manhood. He lay back, swallowed and lost in the rapture of attainment. It was cold, bitter cold, but he did not know it. A shiver or two went through him. He had forgotten Alister, or the fact that Alister lived. Though weariness was on him, it was not the dismayed agony of giddiness. He was exhausted, but he could rest, looking at the swans. Farther and farther he leaned back upon his rowan. He weakened, but his weakness did not trouble him. Darkness came over his sight, but as it blotted out his physical vision there rose somewhere in his consciousness an exhilarating rush—though he was blinded, with some unknown faculty he could see. . . . He was among the swans, and yet he knew dimly that he was still lying on the ground. They were over him, around him, so that he saw the soft yellow shadows under their down, the silver light on their strong feathers . . . yet they were there, over the water, out on the blue ice. . . .

The chill glory that enwrapped both him and them pressed upon his heart. How had he never known before what strange things there were in the world? . . . How had he ever believed that he was old and crippled? . . . How had he never felt what it was to be sucked into the very core of life? With a sudden, ardent effort he sat up, throwing his arms forward, and then fell back.

When Alister neared home he saw his mother standing in the road with Maria. She had returned from Arbroath, having got there to discover that the shops were shut: and now she had made a worse discovery; for Strachan's door was locked and the place empty. She was terribly put about, and the boy could hear the anger in her raised voice. He was in a dreadful position. If he went back to fetch the old man now, he would prove his own guilt; if he stayed away, he would certainly never see the remaining half of its price. In any case the secret must come out, and Strachan, himself discovered, would inevitably reveal his help. The sooner Strachan was got home the better, and he would go and apply for the shilling to-morrow.

"Hae ye seen Maister Strachan, callant?" Maria shouted as he came up.

"Aye, he's awa' tae get a sicht o' yon birds."

They were soon pushing through the whins of the loan, Maria and a couple of men who had come up. Alister followed some way after; instinct told him to keep clear of Maria. When they passed through the

61

beech wood he saw her rush forward and, hearing her loud outcry, he almost turned and fled.

But he did not flee. Cowering among the trees he realised that the part he had played would lie for ever hidden.

With awed curiousity he stole up to the little group. The four stood looking down at Strachan. At last the silence was broken.

"He looks fine an' pleased," said Alister MacHugh.

⟶• Madame Chardinet •⟵

That part of France which passengers in trains look on between Rouen and Paris fascinated Godfrey Barter. It had lived in his mind, in his dreams of the things he liked to think of, during years of work and absence, though it had never occurred to him to consider it as a goal. His life had been contented and busy, yet the picture he would sometimes conjure up lay in him like a photographic plate ready to be developed. The Seine, curving and turning, losing itself in the grey and green and indigo of the land, creeping up again slowly from nowhere, seeming ever brimfull, on the verge of drowning the levels at its sides; in spring, the groups of ethereal bare poplars, their tops touched with warm buff, so fine, so frail that they almost melted into the light. Mantes, with the contours of its ecclesiastical buildings, like a vision; the small towns, scarcely more than overgrown villages, white and grey and dun colour; he had forgotten nothing. The line cut through one of these without disturbing its quiet. He remembered this one particularly.

Barter belonged to the race of Ugly Ducklings, though as a modified specimen. His fortunes had been less brilliant than the fortunes of those advertisements for divine justice and his personality less mean, for, from an ordinary-looking boy he had turned into an upstanding and attractive man. Neither had his parents treated him cruelly, though they had preferred his brothers so distinctly that he had been rather shouldered out of the domestic group. But he had not pined, after the traditional manner of his colleagues, because his godmother, a powerful beldame with a house in the aforesaid small town on the railway, had, from his earliest and callowest schooldays claimed his company for the holidays and franked him from England to France and back again.

No fancied likeness to a dead son nor pity for unrecognised merit had influenced the old lady. She merely preferred the society of boys to that of any other human beings. Their very rascality appealed to her and

63

their directness of outlook. Godfrey fished and climbed, got lifts in barges and loitered about the roads joining himself to carts and pedlars, and would not have changed places with anyone he knew. He was never at home, but at Christmas (which his godmother, though an English-woman, always spent in Paris) and at Christmas time, as we know, everybody makes shift to be pleasant to everybody else.

The French he had learned in his boyhood did something for him. At twenty he had the fortune to be picked out of some dozen others by a man who had large business interests in a French colony, and he was shipped overseas to its main branch. Here, he succeeded so well that, at forty, his good sense and good work, with a leavening of further luck, had given him an interest in the firm. At forty-two, he had a legacy—not from his godmother, for she had been dead some years—and these things considered, he realised that he was on the way to being a rich man. He had been back in England from time to time and it occurred to him that he would like to go home and "look round", perhaps settle there, perhaps marry. Anyhow, he was independent and could do what he liked. And what he had done, before anything else, was to run over to Paris, where business took him as well as pleasure. He loved France.

He sat in the *fumoir* of a Paris hotel looking idly over the newspaper he had picked up from the table at his elbow. The spring sun was on the street and his mind went out of the city into the country and along the railway line to the little town.

It is always startling when something outside one corresponds to one's hidden thoughts. The name of the place he was in, mentally, lay printed under his eye. Among the notices he had read that his godmother's house was for sale. It was to be put up to auction in a week.

He had always meant to go down and see it and he would go soon—at once. Though he knew *Les Marronniers* to have changed hands at least twice since the days he had spent in it and though he supposed that many alterations had been made he hated to think how unlike itself it would surely look after a sale. Everything would be tramped over and covered with litter. He would go tomorrow. He always remembered it as it was in spring, and now he would be seeing it at the right time.

As he got out of the train next day it seemed to him that he had never been away. Everything was so familiar and had been in his mind so long; and though he had forgotten some bits of the way to *Les Marronniers* and new houses had sprung up here and there, in the main, it was wonderfully little changed. Yes, it was the right time to come back.

Over the tops of walls surrounding the older fashioned houses fruit trees were lifting their boughs and through green gates he could see the lilacs; lilacs everywhere, just as they used to be. He stepped along the straggling thoroughfare which could hardly be called a street. There were a few small shops along it, like little vulgar upstarts, but the dwelling houses with their high roofs and green *jalousies* dominated it still; faded plaster and iron gates à *deux battants*. The post office had changed its quarters and the ropemaker whose operations used to enthrall him was gone altogether.

He turned down the side road to get to *Les Marronniers*, which was on the outskirts of everything, and all at once stopped dead; someone he had nearly forgotten was there, before him, across the way. Madame Chardinet! How was it possible that anyone—anything not inanimate—could so remain unchanged, undisturbed? Even the feeling she had produced in his boyish mind sprang upon him again. He shuddered internally.

She was knitting still; her needles flashed in the sun and her black handkerchief was tied tightly round her head. As a child, he had heard that judges condemning murderers to death put on "the black cap" and he had always thought of Madame Chardinet's black handkerchief.

Always, she had seemed to him very old, even older than the middle-aged seem to children, so that now, to the eye of his mature manhood, time had stood still with her. The narrow eyes were a little more sunken under the lowering brows and had the same stare. Some hateful, latent thing haunted her whole personality, as surely as it had done when he was a boy. It is often impossible to be certain when expression is the result of facial structure and when of the spirit within the flesh and bones, and many good souls have suffered because of that impossibility. As a man, Barter knew that; as a boy, he had never been aware of such a difficulty. He was inclined to give Madame Chardinet the benefit of the doubt in spite of his shudder.

He had loathed her though they had never exchanged a word. He had had so many friends from the ropemaker upwards and downwards, but he had never dreamed of speaking to Madame Chardinet. He was anything but bad-hearted yet he had taken her evilness entirely for granted and his feeling had all the force of imagined rectitude behind it. There is an extraordinary priggishness in some small children, drawn from their elders. He had known from his earliest years that he was expected to dislike Satan, which he found rather hard to do, seeing that—from what nurse said—they had so many tastes in common; but he had been quite anxious to do right.

"Ought I to hate wicked people?" he had once asked the ruler of the nursery.

"Oh yes, dear," said she, delighted to see signs of Christianity at such a tender age.

Though he had been lukewarm about Satan there had been no difficulty about Madame Chardinet. He was only nine and, like many other solitary children, he would tell himself long stories about imaginary people. The only real one was Madame Chardinet; she was always the villain of his tales, the one who got worsted in the end. He invented dreadful happenings to her. She would be run over by trains, fall into the hands of man-eating savages, or be struck down in her wickedness by one of his heroes. She never escaped. He recalled these things with a sense of shame and he was glad, even at this distance of time, that he had never told these childish follies to a living soul. No one had known that he was aware of Madame Chardinet's existance.

She looked up across the road at Godfrey. He had changed far more that she had and there was nonrecognition in the look. Though she had seen him pass her door hundreds of times it was small wonder that she did not recognise the lanky boy in the well-set-up man with his short, pointed beard.

Barter went on and was soon at the gate of *Les Marronniers*. It was ajar and the garden empty but for the placard with *"A vendre"* on it which looked stupidly at him from its post, like a clownish, inhospitable face. The tall house with its discoloured plaster and grey *jalousies* had not been altered. No tenant had added to or subtracted anything from its exterior. The round plot of grass before it was unmown but intact, the circular steps to the entrance had the same crack in the lowest step which used to harbour a tiny root of speedwell; the iron bell under its canopy crowning the roof was there too. It had struck awe into his spirit when he first saw it and heard it spoken of as "the fire bell", and later he almost longed to set *Les Marronniers* on fire that he might hear the clamour of its warning. Though he had many times during his first stay begged earnestly to be allowed to ring it, the only result had been that the rope, which hung through a hole in the roof to appear on the topmost landing, had been tied up out of his reach. The horse-chestnuts that gave the place its name were in full flower and as an occasional puff of wind swayed the green of their vivid foliage, the sunlight danced in them and made their white candles glimmer through the shadows of noon.

A ground floor window was open and he looked in. There was a woman in the room sweeping it out with a besom. She considered him suspiciously and stopped, her hands on her hips.

He asked to be let in and her suspicion deepened, so he took a five franc note out of his pocket-book. She came nearer. Who was he, she asked, and what did he want?

He replied that he had heard the house was for sale and that he wished to see it.

Had he a permission? The notary, Monsieur Leduc, might give him one, but he must go and ask him for it. That was the proper thing to do, especially for strangers.

For answer, Barter swung his leg over the sill and got in.

"I used to stay in this house when Madame Barrington lived here," said he.

The name conveyed something to her and she hesitated.

He held out two five franc notes and she took them, reflecting that, as he was already inside and she could not eject him, it would be as well to get some profit out of the episode.

Barter went through the house from top to bottom, opening cupboard doors, stopping at remembered corners. Though it was empty, each aspect of it brought something back to him.

Now, as he stood, gazing through the panes of his old room with the waving foliage, he knew what had been in his mind, unconfessed even to himself, since the moment he had seen the advertisement.

He would buy *Les Marronniers*. It might be an extravagance, but he could afford it. If he liked he could come into the English branch of his business, and though he would have to live in London, he could cross the Channel continually; *Les Marronniers* would be his rest house and he would content himself with very modest rooms in England. He would have to put in some respectable Frenchwoman as caretaker, who would keep the house clean and cook for him. His books should be transferred here and all the possessions that he liked best; there would be a man too, to see to the garden. Should he marry, it would be delightful to watch his children enjoying the same scenes he had enjoyed; but he did not believe he would marry, for he had been too long a bachelor and was too fond of his liberty. He told himself that it was indeed a comfort to have no one who must be consulted on an occasion like the present one; no one to give good advice or say, "Don't."

He went downstairs and out to find Monsieur Leduc. Passing the placard, he looked contemptuously at it, thinking how soon it would be put out of the garden, like any other trespasser.

There had been a lawyer, Leduc, in his day and he felt sure that the person the woman had spoken of must be a son or a nephew—old Leduc, whom he remembered more than twenty years ago, was fat and apoplectic-looking and well over sixty. If he was alive he must have retired by this time. As he was ushered into the office a few minutes later, he remarked that the Leduc in possession was fat too. He was received with much courtesy.

When Barter had explained his position the two men sat on talking. Leduc was of the expansive type and listened with great interest. His uncle, the old man, had been dead many years, he informed Barter, and when he took his place, Mrs Barrington was still living in *Les Marronniers*.

"*Une femme comme il y en a peu!*" exclaimed the lawyer, spreading out his fingers.

Barter rose as the church clock struck mid-day. His train would leave in half an hour said his companion; he proposed that he should go with him to the station, first finishing their cigarettes in the little garden seen through the office window. There was no use in starting till nearer train-time. They transferred themselves to the bench in the spring sunshine.

Barter enjoyed that half hour. He was in the humour for reminiscence and he listened while his host poured out the history of nearly every creature and every episode that had happened in the place since he came to it. The guest urged him on; now that he was hoping to be part of the local life every word was of interest to him. It was like re-reading some cherished book that had been lost. His mind, which took fire easily from an idea, was already settling in the surroundings that attracted him so much.

"There is one person left whom I know by sight," he said at last, "Madame Chardinet."

"Ah—Madame Chardinet. The one who lives near *Les Marronniers*. Yes. She is very old. She must be nearly eighty."

It was on the tip of Barter's tongue to ask what he knew about her. He would have liked to ask what sort of character she bore among her neighbours.

But he held his peace, for his own foolishness as a boy seemed now so much more foolish; in any case he could not change it nor make the other understand it if he did. It was evident that Leduc saw nothing unusual in her.

They strolled together to the station. The Frenchman's tongue had not had such an outing for months. They had settled every detail about the coming auction. He was to expect Barter on the day it would take place and they would go to it together; also he was to engage and instruct the man who would do the bidding for his client. Very few people had come to see the place. He would do the legal business consequent upon the taking over of *Les Marronniers*, should Barter be successful; and he had made a note of the last price to which the latter was prepared to go.

"I hope I shan't be disappointed," said Barter out of the train window as they parted.

"Fear nothing," said Leduc, pursing his lips archly. "You will see. All will go well."

He had been considerably astonished at Barter's figures.

Godfrey was pretty busy during the following week and, in the lucid intervals of business matters the thought of his coming venture cropped up pleasantly.

Three days before the auction he had a wire from his sister in England begging him to come home at once. Their father, a widower over seventy and lying ill from a serious heart attack, was longing for the presence of one of his sons. He had not seen much of Godfrey during his lifetime, but the other two were overseas, one in India and one in New Zealand. Miss Barter urged her only brother within reach to come as quickly as possible, for no one knew how the illness might end, nor how soon.

There was nothing to be done but go and Barter set off, writing to tell Leduc what had happened and asking him to wire the result of the sale.

As he whirled along between Dover and London the faint sunshine above was cold and everything that grew was a stage behind France. He revered and admired his country and would have gone to the stake for all it stood for but its aspect chilled him. He had lived too long abroad to feel anything but a general pride in his birthright; in the distance, the idea of living at home had been attractive but it was different at close quarters. He had wavered, but there was no more wavering. It was *Les Marronniers* for him.

"I'm glad to tell you father is very much better," said his sister as she met him on the platform of a little country station.

"That's a good thing," he said, rather stupidly.

Eleanor was almost a stranger to him and he had forgotten how like a cabhorse she was.

Decency obliged him to propose a week's stay and he resigned himself. Though his thoughts were principally of the expected news from France he made himself as useful as he could. Many neighbours came to enquire for old Mr Barter and the female part of them was duly entertained by his daughter. Godfrey carried chairs and plates of cake and teacups and was consistently polite to a type of human being of which he had no experience. "Do they dress from a sense of humour or the lack of it?" he wondered. The day of the sale came. He had said nothing of it to his family and in the afternoon he loitered about outside the gates, smoking and keeping watch for the telegraph boy. At last the bicycle appeared between the hedges. Leduc, who always spoke French with Godfrey, had written his message in English for the benefit of the English post office.

"Very grief, none success".

Barter hastened back across the Channel next day all immediate danger to his father's life being over, but a new terror had occurred to him. Should the old man's precarious life suddenly end and his sister be left alone, she might suggest that, as the only unmarried members of the family, they should live together. He felt he would do anything for anybody, short of setting up house with Eleanor. She would certainly never leave England, therefore he would be safer abroad. So he went back to Paris to consider his plans and see Leduc, for he longed to know how he had lost what both had considered so safe.

The lawyer wrote that he was coming up to Paris soon and Godfrey asked him to dinner.

"What a misfortune!" exclaimed the Frenchman, as they shook hands, "And I, who had counted on so good a neighbour!"

"Sit down," said Barter. "Dinner isn't ready yet. I want to hear everything."

"I was there," began Leduc, drawing his chair up close. "Before the gate was opened for the auctioneer I was there. There were some of our own people, not come to buy to see—*pour s'amuser, enfin.* I was happy, smiling. I laughed, thinking of the sum written down in my book. M. Bartaire may content himself, I thought, with half of that. It was not quick, the affair. It went very slow. I had commanded Dumont not to engage himself till I had made him the little sign we had arranged between us. I would not begin too soon. I waited till there were only two left to contend—a man from Amiens and a stranger. Then I laid my finger against my nose and Dumont began. The man from Amiens stopped but the stranger continued. When they had come to twenty-five thousand francs the stranger seemed to hesitate. I said to myself, "It will not be long! We have it. It is in my pocket. Dumont cried 'twenty-six!' and the stranger turned away. Before the auctioneer could open his mouth

Madame Chardinet pushed herself to the front. I had not seen her till that moment. I did not suppose she was there. I was amazed; she stood facing Dumont, bidding him up. He had hardly time to breathe. She was *épouvantable*—horrible! What eyes! What a face! A she-devil—an animal. None could imagine what had come to her. My heart sank as they approached our sum. I said, "I will add ten when Dumont stops. M. Bartaire will understand. Not more, I can do no more."

The time came when Dumont stopped and I spoke.

"She gave me the look of an assassin. Then she bid over my price. *Et voila! Fini.*"

Barter sat still without a word.

"Is Madame Chardinet rich?" he said at last.

"Comfortable, without doubt—but no more. She must make many sacrifices to pay for her madness. And what can she want with *Les Marronniers*, she who has a good house that she has inhabited all her life and not a child to inherit it? I said to Dumont 'She is mad—crazy.' '*Possédée*', he said, '*c'est une possédée.*' "

Barter lay awake that night turning over Leduc's story. What was the meaning of what had happened, the meanings below the surface facts? It seemed that now, for the first time, Madame Chardinet had come into prominence, for apparently no one had given more heed to her than to any other old woman living in the place; he alone had found anything in her to remark. Now, her appearance at the sale, the price she had paid, and above all, her sensational excitement, was discussed from one end of the little town to another.

"It was almost as if she hated English people," Leduc had said, "but I do not believe it was that. There was no difficulty between her and Madame Barrington, I think?"

Barter shook his head. He had a theory, though it was too wild to accept, even in the recesses of his soul, where what a man's brain rejects will sometimes find a place. Was it possible that thought, hidden deep, let loose from one mind, can settle in that of another? He had wondered how Madame Chardinet could know for whom Dumont was bidding, that is, if she *did* know; but that question did not puzzle him long, for in spite of Leduc's official secrecy, he was sure that nothing known to him could remain long hidden: But that she *did* know, Barter was certain, with a quite indefensible certainty. He lay amazed, nonplussed. Madame had had her revenge though not one word of his feeling about her had ever, in all his life, passed his lips.

There was nothing left but his theory.

━• The Yellow Dog •━

"Aye, a doag's grand company."

The platitude floated out on the murky air of the smiddy in which three men were smoking; it hung for a minute, unanswered, and the shepherd took his pipe out of his mouth and emitted a solemn "aye".

Outside, the late October afternoon dwindled to evening; work being over, the smith sat on his anvil facing the shepherd and old Robert Spence.

"Grand, grand company," said Spence again.

The blacksmith pushed his cap back. He was very much younger than his companions and perhaps had not outgrown the taste for disagreeing with his elders.

"Weel," he said slowly, "I kent a man—I didna exactly ken him weel, though I kent plenty about him—that wasna just benefited by the company o' a doag."

"It isna ilka body that understands doags," said Spence.

"The man I'm tellin' ye o' was a lang time or he understood ane o' them."

The shepherd made no comment, but the quality of contempt in his silence was a challenge to the smith.

"It was ma wife's uncle," he began, "that had a fairm oot yonder at the fit o' the Sidlaws—a cantankered-like carle that hadna very muckle tae say till onybody. He'd naethin' tae say tae me, at ony rate, for I was coortin' at the time, and the lassie had an awfae wark tae get ootby tae meet me. I daur'd na come near the hoose. Ye see, he was that set against me, but whiles we'd hae a word thegither, her an' me, ahint a dyke, when it was possible. Weel, there was a nicht we was there and we could hear the treid o' a man runnin' an pechin' up the brae and we were fair fleggit, Bell an' me, but the auld deevil gae'd by an' never saw naethin'. He was that pit aboot. Ye could see the heid o'm against the sma' licht there was i' the sky and his hair was tousled an' his bonnet lost."

"Was't a doag chasin' him?" asked Spence.

"Na, na—but listen you till I tell ye—it had been him chasin' a doag—"

"The fule," broke in the shepherd.

"Ye micht think that, perhaps. But I mind when Bell got the chance tae tell me the richts o' it, I was whiles fear'd tae gang oot i' the dairk ma lane—aye was I."

"Feech!" exclaimed the shepherd, "ye were owre young tae be oot late—coortin' tae! Ye're no muckle mair nor a laddie the noo."

"I'm a married man this twa year," rejoined the smith, "and there's a wean at hame and anither comin'. But that's nae matter. Mind you what I'm tae tell ye. It'll gar ye think. Yon man, Bell's uncle, had got sheep awa' up upo' the hill and he'd been oot seekin' a yowe that was missin' frae the flock."

At the mention of a flock the shepherd's humour began to change and the two old men fixed their eyes on the smith's face.

"Aye, he was up amang the hills an' he couldna get word o' the yowe and he was fair done, what wi' traiv'lin' the bogs he didna ken, an' trampin' a' kind o' places an' duntin' himsel' amang the stanes. It was i' the autumn, a day like this; the afternoon was gettin' on an' he couldna see whaur he was, for he was newly come tae the fairm and he wasna accustomed tae the hills. He was a Fife body. I'se warrant ye he said some queer things, for he was an ill-tongued man, and at last he thocht he wadna fash himsel' ony mair wi' the yowe an' just leave the bizzer tae dee in her sins. Forbye there was a pucklie mist, and it was takin' him a' his time tae win doon tae ceevilization or sunset.

"At last he got his feet on the flat ground and he cam' upon a warld o' whins; there wasna a hoose nor a beast tae be seen, an' when he was through the whins it was the same; naethin' but a muckle green place wi' clumps o' rashes and ne'er a peewee nor a whaup tae cry owre his heid. He was standin' like a fule when a dairk-like thing cam oot frae ahint a tree-stump aboot as far aheid as he micht see, an' it had the appearance o' a doag. It cam' towards him wi' its heid doon an' he could tell through the gloamin' that it was a kind o' a yella colour; its tail was hangin' atween its legs. It lookit queer, he thocht. (Man, I dinna like thae things!)"

He paused for breath; the old men said nothing, for the smith was transporting them into places whose like they had seen many a time.

"It cam' and stoppit a wee bittie in front o' him; syne it startit rinnin' roond him. Whiles it ran in a muckle circle, whiles in sma' anes. But aye it ran; roond an' round wi' its heid hangin', and whiles it lookit up at him wi' its yella een, whiles no. He couldna say what tae mak' o' it, but it seemed as if the cratur kent somethin' that gar'd it behave yon way. His he'rt was like tae dee, he said, yon thing had that ill look aboot it; he tried strikin' oot wi' his stick, but he couldna reach it, and at last he just steppit forrit though he didna ken the road he was takin'; a' he thocht was tae get rid o' the brute. But it was nae use, for it gae'd on afore him, turnin' its heid an' lookin' back tae see if he was comin'. He stude still when he saw that and the doag commenced tae rin round him the same as before. Whatever he tried, he couldna get quit o'm."

"I dinna believe ye," said Spence.

"I'm no' carin'," replied the smith, "but I can haud ma tongue gin ye like. Am I tae gang on?"

Spence and the shepherd put their pride in their pockets, and the smith continued.

"Weel, it cam' intill the man's mind that the beast micht be makin' for its hame, and gin he was to folla it he'd maybe land at some hoose whaur he'd get put on his road, so he began to think shame o' himsel' for no seein' that it was just a nat'ral thing, and awa' they went, him an' the doag. There was bogs an' ditches, broom an' tracks runnin' in and oot o' the lang grass, amangst the black shaws o' the weepies that was deein' i' the autumn. He didna ken foo lang they'd traivelt, and gin he stude tae tak's breith the thing afore him wad stap an' turn back, and though he tell't himsel' that a doag was a doag and nae mair, he couldna thole the notion o' it comin' near an' maybe runnin' roond him again. There wasna a body tae be seen nor a man's voice tae hear as they gaed ane ahint the ither, but at last the doag loupit through a broken place whaur the stanes had whummled oot o' a dyke on till a road. It was a narra road and there was a bittie green grass at the side o' it, and he was fine an' pleased when he saw it, for he kent it, and yonder no' far aheid was the muckle grey stane that stickit up like the figure o' a man, by the arn trees i' the weet ditch. He wasna mair nor a mile frae hame and the kent, nat'ral look o't made him bauld, the same as a suppie whusky micht hae done, and anger't him aye the mair at the doag though it had brocht him sae far on his journey. As I tell't ye, he was a thrawn cratur and he up an' hurled his stick and struck the beast i' the side. It didna cry nor rin; it just cam' back till him and ran a great circle roond him. He didna like that and he saw he'd get nae peace till he was at his ain door and could clap it i' the doag's face; sae he gaed on again, an' it rinnin' afore him, and as they passed the stane amang the arn trees the beast stoppit that quick he was near steppin' on it. He lookit doon tae his feet, and it was gone. There was nae doag there."

"Nae doag there?" cried the shepherd.

"Aye, naethin'. There was naethin'. The road was toom but for himsel', and he was that terrified that he started awa' wi' the cauld sweit drippin' on his cheeks and ran till his breith was done. That was the nicht Bell an' me saw him come hame."

The smith stopped and looked at his companions.

"Noo, what div ye mak' o' that?" he asked, as neither of them spoke.

"I wad say that yon man had been a leear," replied the shepherd judicially; "and, ony way, it's time I was awa'. Come on, min."

The collie rose at the summons and followed his master to the door.

The smith turned to Spence.

"Ah weel, ye see," said the old man. "I wasna there mysel, and I couldna exactly say . . ."

He began to bestir himself too.

"But will ye no bide and hear the end o' it?" called the smith to the shepherd's back, which, square and heavy, filled the doorway.

"An' is that no' the end?"

"Na, there's mair."

The young man had not moved from the anvil; but the shepherd, though he turned round, stayed in the doorway; to have approached would have been a concession to folly, to youth, to all sorts of officially negligible things.

"It was a while after when I got this job here an' was married," began the smith again. "I was acquaint wi' yon business o' the doag and we'd speak aboot it at times, her an' me. But the man himsel' couldna thole tae hear aboot it, for there was some that made a joke o't an' wad cry oot when he passed, *'Whaur's yer doag, Fifie? Hae ye gi'en him a holiday?'* But there wasna very muckle use for him tae be pretendin' wi' us that had seen him yon nicht comin' hame dementit-like, and Bell had been i' the hoose and got the tale frae his ain lips. But we said naethin' tae upset him, and noo that the lassie an' me was man an' wife, and the smiddy daein' weel, he didna tak sae ill at me, and we'd gang tae the fairm, noo and again, o' Sawbaths, for her auntie likit Bell.

"It was on ane o' thae days that we was there. There was just the auntie at hame, for her man had gane awa' aifter the kirk was oot and tell't her he wad be hame for tea time. A braw November day it was, saft and freish, and I mind we went oot i' the yaird when dinner was done, for Bell had wrocht wi' the turkey when she was at fairm and was seekin' tae see what like birds her auntie had gotten this year. The turkey-hens were steppin' aboot an' the bubblyjock scrapin' his wings alang the ground because I was whustlin' at him tae gar him rage; we was lauchin' at him when a little lassie lookit ower the palin' an' cried on us.

"'Mistress Donal'! Mistress Donal'! Yer man tell't me tae come for ye, for he's no verra weel—he's got a sair pain in his he'rt an' he canna stand. He bad me mak' haste. He's doon this way!"

"We a' set aff, and the lassie brocht us tae the same road that he'd traiv'led wi' the doag mair nor a year syne. Puir Mistress Donald was no' that quick on her feet for she was stoot and no just young, and I left Bell wi' her an' ran. When I got roond a turn I could see the arn trees that were bare but for a wheen broun leaves, wi' the muckle stane stickin' up below them frae the rank grass, an' there was a dark heap lyin' terrible still at the stane's fit.

"It was him, deid. It took me a while tae mak' sure, and when I raised mysel' tae see whether Bell and the puir body was comin', I heard a kind o' movin' an lookit roond.

"Aboot a stane's thraw frae's, there was a yella doag standin' lookin' at me."

77

⟝• Secret Intelligence •⟞

It would, perhaps, have been unkind to call Mr Percy Chudworth Lee-Hickson conceited. It was only when he grew confidential—which the best of us are apt to do at times—that he talked much about himself. And younger men, with whom he adopted the paternal attitude (he was forty-three) were sometimes impressed by him.

"Yes," he said one afternoon to a young fellow of his acquaintance, a clerk in the House of Commons, "I don't pretend to be a genius, but I keep my eyes open and my ears too. Very little escapes me, I can tell you. I'm like a hound—put me on the scent and I'll get there somehow. Now, my mind's never sleeping—it's always on the look out. I look into the reasons of things—the causes. It's good practice. You young fellows don't appreciate that; but none of the little signs of all that goes on are ever lost on me. I'm a sort of 'mind-scout', you might say."

"Are you supposed to do one kind action a day?" enquired the youth who was a little flippant, "because, if you are, you might try one on me."

"Well, so I will," said Mr Lee-Hickson, who saw enough to suspect that he was having his leg pulled, "I shall advise you not to wear such loud socks." Mr Lee-Hickson, himself, dressed quietly; in summer principally in blue serge. He was of middle height, fair and slender and a little bald; he strove with the baldness by means of hairwashes and by the careful training of his hair, which he applied to the thin places as though he were training Virginia Creeper. He lived in the country but was well enough off to make occasional visits to London, which he loved dearly, and as he was a bachelor, it may be presumed that he was free from cares. His home, on the outskirts of a South Country cathedral town, was a pattern of comfort. He was a good croquet player, an ardent collector of Welsh pewter and he had just bought a small motor-car. All these things pleased him and the knowledge of his own sagacity made a comfortable undercurrent to his life.

The young man with the loud socks attempted no further flippancies and the next time that Mr Lee-Hickson made reference to his own discernment, he took a different tone.

"You should go into the secret service," he said; "that's the place for you. You'd be invaluable. Why don't you apply to be taken on?"

This time Mr Lee-Hickson had no misgivings. He felt the words to be so true that he did not suspect his companion of grinning internally at the thought of anyone of his appearance engaged in desperate deeds.

He smiled darkly.

"Well," he said, "perhaps I have done so—who knows?"

He went home from the county club, where this conversation had taken place, in a reflective mood, for Ernest Darton had only voiced his own thoughts, his own convictions. Even that young ass had perceptions, it seemed, and he smoked among his pewter that evening, wondering whether destiny had been speaking to him through this unworthy medium.

He thought about it in bed, at breakfast, for days afterwards, and finally came to the tremendous resolution. He had always been interested in matters of intrigue and he knew that the secret service was recruited from every conceivable branch of society. People of position and people of none; people of both sexes and of all grades and professions formed part of the vast web spun round the unsuspecting public by those responsible for its safety. Why not himself? Even Henri Le Caron had, presumably, not been born with secret orders in his hand. There is a beginning to everything; and so Mr Lee-Hickson told himself many times in the couple of weeks that ensued before he made the plunge. And, one day, having decided to what official he should apply, he posted his letter. He gave the history of his own antecedents and position, and the capabilities which he knew himself to possess, asking to be employed (as a beginning) in even the most humble capacity. He then set about possessing his soul in patience until his deed should take effect.

Weeks passed with no result. It was a little over a month from the day of his resolution when a most unassuming envelope with a London postmark lay upon the table when he came in one night to dress for dinner. He opened it with a sigh; it looked so like a bill. It had neither date, address, nor signature, and it was only when he had read it through that the meaning of its contents dawned upon him.

"On the 18th inst," the letter ran, "you will proceed to Ford Lane Station, on the Great Eastern line, arriving there before 6.10 p.m., when a local train due at that hour will come in on a branch line. A tall lady will arrive by it accompanied by a small King Charles spaniel. She will take the 6.25 to Harwich. You will find means to prevent her from starting by that train. <u>Urgent</u>" (the word was thrice underlined) Destroy. <u>You have been under consideration for some time.</u>"—

Mr Lee-Hickson stood thunderstruck. Here it was, the long-expected letter! It had come upon him so stealthily, with so little pomp or circumstance that it took him a few minutes to collect his wits and screw up his feelings to the occasion. He had imagined something quite different. There was no proposed interview, no producing himself for inspection. Then, as he told himself how unlikely it was that an urgent secret order would carry its origin on its face, he began to wonder at his own astonishment.

The last sentence made his head buzz. Was it an explanation of the tardy reply, or did it mean that omniscient eyes had followed him, weighing his merits, even before he had taken action? *Was he known?* It was a giddy thought!

Today was the 17th. Mr Lee-Hickson swallowed his dinner in a dream, and when this was done, he burned the letter, making cryptic notes of its contents, then went to find Bradshaw. He looked up the trains mentioned and saw that he could get to London quite comfortably and spend a pleasant few hours before starting for Ford Lane.

He began to construct some probable situation from what he had been told. Evidently the lady was going abroad and crossing from Harwich, and for some unaccountable reason, it was imperative to delay her; it was a political matter, of course—heaven knew what might not depend on his success! He was rather surprised to see that the missing of that particular train would not prevent her from sailing that evening, but, like a wise man, he questioned nothing for which he was not responsible and concluded that there was no need for him to understand more than his orders. He spent the evening in a chastened attitude, shadowed by the faint fear of being unsuccessful. Not that he really felt incapable of dealing with any matter. It was merely the preliminary shiver of the expert swimmer on the brink.

He departed for London next day, composed and resolute, having put together a rough plan of action. The dog was the key to the situation. If its mistress carried anything of vital importance she would certainly not part from it for a single moment, and he felt that the best means of delaying her would be to detain some of her property. A woman (so he reasoned) is always a slave to her pet dog, and so, by some contrivance, he must lay hands on the little beast. Short of breaking her leg, or taking her purse, he could see no other way out of it. Being a devoted admirer of ladies, the first was abhorrent to him, and unless some miracle should happen there would be no chance of getting hold of her money. Of course he might try to steal her purse, but the thought of being taken up as a pickpocket was too much for his courage. Better to retire once more into obscurity than that. Should he manage to get hold of her ticket and should she only discover its loss in the train, no end would be served, for she would only have to make it good on the journey. No, unless some amazing chance presented itself, it was the dog. The waiter who served him in the Lyons restaurant in which he lunched was astonished, when removing his plate, to see that though the gentleman had eaten two small cutlets, there was only one bone left.

At last the time came when Mr Lee-Hickson was at Liverpool Street, stepping into the train. He had not spent a pleasant afternoon, for the greasy bone in his coat pocket was offensive to him and he had kept out of any known haunt of his own for fear of meeting acquaintances who might ask awkward questions, or, worse still, be going his way. He had no connection with the East of England, but one never knows one's luck in this world; certainly never one's ill-luck.

As he sat in his empty compartment with his unread evening paper, he wondered, rather sadly, whether the next day's issue would hold his own name, whether he might get into some hideous difficulty, only to be the sport of the evening paper, only to have his face pictured next Sunday—heavens, how horribly! in the spicy columns of *The News of the World*!

At last the train pulled up at Ford Lane station and he got out. It was a little place, with the branch line he had heard of running in on the other side of the platform, which made a sort of peninsula between the main and the lesser line. There was a covered booking office and a small waiting room, and, far up the further end of the platform, under the shadow of a bridge that carried the high road over the permanent way, was a nondescript wooden shed with a few oil-lamps propped against it. There was only one porter, who stirred himself into temporary activity when trains came in.

Mr Lee-Hickson laid the suitcase that he carried as a guarantee of travellership upon a bench; before starting, he had emptied it of everything that could give a clue to his identity. He informed the porter that he was going by the 6.25 and then proceeded to loiter up and down, taking stock of all that he saw. He walked as far the bridge and noted the little shed, smiling as he saw that the key was in the door. When some little time had been spent in looking about he saw the signal go down on the branch line, and with a beating heart, turned his steps with what nonchalance he could to the place where the incoming train would draw up.

Soon a puff of smoke showed round a curve and the small train came clanking in. The third-class doors opened, disgorging a handful of country folk, and from the only first-class compartment there descended a tall, elegant figure, dressed in brown, with an up-to-date hat on its head and a little spaniel under its arm.

Mr Lee-Hickson's heart beat like a drum as he watched the lady directing the porter, who was hauling a small trunk and a huge hat-box from the van. He could hear her telling the man that she was going by the 6.25 to Harwich.

To his immense relief the third class passengers, one and all, filed out and took the road to the small town whose houses began to border the road not a quarter of a mile off. Soon the newcomer's luggage had been deposited in a stack outside the ticket office and no one remained in the station but himself and the stranger. He was thankful to see the dog was not on a leash; it was evidently a well-behaved little being, for it trotted quietly after its mistress.

Mr Lee-Hickson had heard the porter tell her that the ticket office would not open till ten minutes before the train arrived. Then would be the critical moment; then, when she was buying her ticket, would be the time for the deed he had to do. So far, the ground seemed to prepare well. He strolled up and down, his hands in his pockets; the porter had gone off up the road to a little cottage, evidently his own, and, no doubt, would return in time for the 6.25.

The lady sat on a bench beside the usual wayside station flowerbeds and the dog, running about, sniffed at Mr Lee-Hickson's heels as he passed on his quarter-deck walk. He stooped and patted it, and as his fingers had just been in contact with the bone in his pocket, it licked his hand and then followed him a little way. It was a good beginning.

At last the hands of Mr Lee-Hickson's watch pointed to 6.15, ten minutes before train-time.

The dusk was creeping on, but now that he was so close upon action, he had grown calm. He was only a few steps from the lady when she rose and turned towards the office, opening her bag.

Once more fortune favoured the brave, for she passed Mr Lee-Hickson, who found himself between her and the dog. The little creature was midway between himself and the lamp-house by the bridge. At the sight of its mistress walking away it came running back and approached Mr Lee-Hickson just as the lady disappeared into the office.

He snatched the bone from his pocket and held it out to the dog. It stopped, sniffed, took the delicious morsel in its teeth and was lost.

At a breathless run the triumphant man carried it up the platform. It struggled, but held tightly to the bone, while Mr Lee-Hickson, smothering it with his pocket-handkerchief, made what speed he could. He just managed to knot the silk over its head and round its neck before he reached the lamp-house. Opening the door, he shot the spaniel into the darkness, shut it, turning the key, which he dropped into his pocket, and went back, panting but exultant, down the platform. He prayed that distance and the folds of his fine bandana would strifle any outcry the innocent animal might make; cheerfully would he have given twenty pounds to be sure that the 6.25 would be up to time.

He came back to find the ticket-office still closed and the lady studying an advertisement on the wall while she waited for it to open. The clock showed that there were still six mintues to train-time. The little ticket-window went up.

Then it was that a great idea occurred to Mr Lee-Hickson. As she came out to the platform, ticket in hand, he took off his hat and accosted her.

"Madam," he said, "your little dog has run away."

"Oh!" she exclaimed, blankly, "Oh, thank you so much! Good heavens! Which way did he go?"

"Out there!" exclaimed Mr Lee-Hickson, pointing to the town. "It rushed up the road after another dog. I did all I could—I whistled—you must have heard me?"

"Indeed, I didn't," said she.

"Through that little gate, out into the road; that's the way it went," continued he.

"It's too dreadful! cried she, dropping her arms at her sides. "I must hunt for him at once. What *shall* I do if my train comes in before I find him?"

"It won't," said he, looking at his watch and praying that she might not take out hers. "We have a full eight minutes—more, in fact. Shall we go a little way towards the town? The dog will know your call and it won't know mine!"

"We had better run," said she.

So they ran.

She was young and agile and Mr Lee-Hickson had to exert himself to keep up with her. They ran past the porter's cottage and past a little inn, and had got half way to the town before they paused to call and whistle. Then they ran on again. At last they stopped, for there was no sign of the spaniel anywhere. Before them, the street-lamps were beginning to be lit and to spot the dusk. The road rang with calls of "Ruby! Ruby!" and frantic whistling.

"Look at your watch again," she said, panting. "I *mustn't* lose that train."

"It's all right," said he, complying. "Besides they'd surely keep it a moment. They know you're going by it. We have four minutes before we need turn back—Why, there's you dog! look! look! Turning down between those two houses—call again!"

She called with all her might.

"I *can't* see him," she said.

It was well within a minute of train-time.

She ran on a few yards, hesitated, and stopped short.

"It's no good," she exclaimed, "and I must go back. I've simply got to get on!"

She turned, and as she did so, the noise of the approaching train came to her ears. Mr Lee-Hickson had heard it before, but the sound of her own voice and her own whistling had kept it from her.

She began to run back frantically, but they had come further than she supposed and she was breathless from her exertions. She made a gallant run, leaving her companion stranded where he was, but before she had covered half the distance, she fell into walk, keeping all her strength to shout and wave to the porter, who had returned to the platform.

But Ford Lane was a small station and the train had only one minute's wait there. She forced herself to some semblance of a run again, but even as she did so, the guard's green flag went up and the engine started. The train moved out into the dusk to lose itself under the bridge.

In spite of what he had accomplished, the next ten minutes were among the worst of Mr Lee-Hickson's life. His companion was in a state of distraction and it was all she could do to keep within the bounds of civility. He protested that he had not known how much his watch had lost, he abased himself, he cursed himself for his folly, he offered apologies that should have melted a stone; he felt as if drowning in a sea of hypocrisy. She was so attractive, in such a quandary, and he had, in cold blood, put her, as the vulgar say, "in the cart", ruined prospects, perhaps, to which she looked for her livelihood. No wonder she was distraught. No wonder she was resentful! Also, he was far, far from indifferent to the hateful fact that she thought him an absolute fool.

But his cup was not yet drained. There might be worse to come. He had yet to prevent the awful catastrophe of the discovery of the dog. What if the porter should need some implement for the lamphouse? What if he should produce another key or break in the door? What if the spaniel should make some lamentation loud enough to reach its mistress and be found with his silk handkerchief wound tight about its bullet head? Mercifully, her dismay seemed to have overpowered the thought of the lost Ruby, but at any moment, she might remember her pet. Mr Lee-Hickson grew cold at the thought.

There was nothing for it but to brace himself for renewed action. The lady was in the telegraph office, sending a message—a cypher one, no doubt. She had not spoken to him since their return to the station but he felt that he must, at all costs, get her out of the way if he was to see the affair of the dog to its end. Also, he felt that the restoration of the spaniel was the one reparation in his power.

He met her on the threshold of the telegraph office. His idea was to propose to escort her to the inn, where she could get some tea and rest until the next train for Harwich should arrive, while he made a more exhaustive search for the missing Ruby.

It took all the eloquence he could command to make her listen, but at last, after infinite pains, and the endurance of many biting words and allusions, he set forth once more up the road with his scornful companion. This time they did not run; they walked in a strained and bitter silence that galled Mr Lee-Hickson to the soul. He left her in the inn parlour, and refusing to partake of the tea she constrained herself to offer him, he went out into the dusk.

The station was again deserted, but, as it was too dark to see much, it would not have mattered had it been full. Mr Lee-Hickson made a dash towards the bridge, and stopping by the lamphouse, laid his ear to the door. Scratching and muffled whining came from within.

Softly he took the heavy key from his pocket and softly the turned it in the lock. As the door opened, a thing like a miniature whirlwind dashed at his legs; he had just time to clap his ankles firmly together and make a dive at the dog before it could dodge round them. He got it by the loose skin of its back and lifted it, struggling, to his arms. His bandana was in ribbons and he had some difficulty in disentangling them from its collar.

Mr Lee-Hickson was a man who liked to do things artistically and the dim light glimmering on a muddy ditch a few paces down the line showed him how to throw a glamour of realism on the episode. In its waters he rolled the outraged Ruby, mopping its shallow bed with the little brute as a housemaid mops a flooded floor. It was not easy to get his victim consistently wet, but he did it at last. Then he started with the spluttering creature for the inn.

He burst into the parlour with the dripping bundle in his arms.

"Ruby!" cried its owner, snatching it from him.

"Poor little animal!" exclaimed Mr Lee-Hickson; "no wonder it did not come to your whistle! It had fallen headlong into a bottomless ditch beyond the railway bridge and it was making the most pitiful efforts to get out when I heard it cry. I am thankful I thought of going in that direction. It must have rushed back when I saw it turn down behind the houses."

She overwhelmed him with thanks. As he met her eyes he saw that she had employed some of her time in crying.

"And now," he said, "you will be all right here waiting for the 6.51, so I will leave you. I am so infinitely relieved to have found you dog, after all the trouble I have caused you. You may forgive me, but I shall never be able to forgive myself."

He spoke with a melancholy dignity—the dignity of one whose misfortune is greater than his fault—and left her.

The propitious sight of the porter back on the platform greeted him as he reached the station.

"Is there a London train due soon?" he asked, breathlessly; "if not, where can I get a motorcar, or a carriage, or a bicycle, or a—"

"'Ere be the 6.37 a' comin' in, just signalled," said the man.

"Thank God!" exclaimed Mr Lee-Hickson.

* * *

Having some experience of official delays Mr Lee-Hickson was prepared to wait calmly for the recognition of his services, and it was a week after his exploit that he walked into the County Club, well-pleased with life and his own part in it. An acquaintance was sitting reading a letter; otherwise the place was empty.

"You seem amused," observed Mr Lee-Hickson, noticing his expression.

"So I am," replied the other. "Ernest Darton has run away with an heiress."

"I am really delighted," said Mr Lee-Hickson, recalling his last conversation with the young man; "he is a very sensible, deserving youth."

"Yes, but listen to this," continued his companion, shaking with

86

laughter. "You see, the girl's people wouldn't have it and they decided to bolt. She was in the North and he was in London and they were to meet at Harwich and cross to Rotterdam together. Well, the day before, he found that he'd be detained in the House of Commons too late to meet her at the time they'd settled. It wasn't safe to wire, and there wasn't time to write, as she'd already started from Wick, or some infernal place, so he got some ass of a fellow to contrive that she should miss her train at a small station and when the next one came in, Darton was in it, and they went off together. The fellow fancied himself as a detective and thought he'd got a commission to do the job from the Secret Service. It's almost too good to be true. Lord! I respect Darton!"

He shook again.

When Mr Lee-Hickson got home there was a foreign letter on the hall table. He opened it to find the photograph of a King Charles spaniel and a visiting card. On the former was written "With fond love from Ruby" and on the latter, "With Mr and Mrs Ernest Darton's compliments!"

"I've paid him for my 'loud socks'," Darton had said, as he posted the letter.

⟵• Anderson •⟶

"Come awa' an' get yer wheeps!"

Anderson Craig MacNichol, who was thus summoned, sat in the yard rubbing down a wooden hobbyhorse, a creature with legs like the handles of hearth-brooms and a strip of fur mane nailed on its flat, semi-circular neck.

Anderson put out his tongue till it almost covered his chin. There was nothing odd in that; children have done the same from time immemorial, but he did it automatically and without so much as raising his eyes to the figure standing at the kitchen door. It was a sufficiently intimidating one too; for Mrs Craig, Anderson's maternal grandmother, was a tall spare beldame and wore a high black cap tied with purple ribbons. It was from her that he had got his middle name; the first one had been given him in honour of an uncle in America. Another thing that had come to him from his grandmother was his long nose, and though his pointed chin and pink and white complexion had a girlish look, it was a misleading one, for, in character, he was Napoleonic and his small blue eyes should have been warning to all who stood in his way.

"Come awa'!" cried the old woman again.

"No me," replied Anderson.

"Did I no tell ye no tae mairter yer guid claes 'yont i' the dirt? Ye'll get the tawse for that. Div ye no hear me?"

"Aye, fine", said he.

She took a step towards him, but only one; for she had felt shoes on and there was an extensive puddle before the door.

He did not move. It was not worth his while.

She turned and went in. Prudence had its place in Anderson's character and he did not know whether his father was about, for it was Sunday. He looked down at the splashes of mud on his nether garments that had been spotless in the morning when his mother had driven him

88

kirkwards before her. Mrs MacNichol was proud of the smug little figure in front, scrubbed and brushed as became the child of a man who farmed seventy acres and kept a horseman for his pair.

Anderson put his hands in his pockets as he had seen the horseman do and was soon out of the yard and on his way down the side road that led to the river. It had rained a good deal and he could hear the South Esk, growling and swollen, pushing its course through the rocks below the bridge. Home was unsuitable to him at the moment and his mind open to anything that should be less so, therefore he saw with pleasure that a group of boys of his own age was gathered a little way on. Here was company and something to put his mind to. He advanced on them with interest; they were coming towards him and they laughed and shouted as they surrounded one of their number. As he neared them one of the crowd ran forward holding up something that writhed and wriggled.

"Hae!" he shouted. "See what we've gotten!"

Anderson stopped as he saw a wretched draggled kitten that miaued and struggled in the boy's grip. The others came pressing round.

"We're tae pit it into yon!" cried one, pointing to a pond that the rain had swollen till it encroached on the wayside, "and we've gaithered stanes tae see wha'll git it the first crack!"

The sight of the little creature held up aloft made Anderson's small eyes grow as hard as marbles. His one weakness was for animals. Even the wooden hobby-horse, that his parents said was a shame for anyone of seven years old to play with, was dear to him because it had its very remote likeness to a beast on four legs. Without further ado he rushed at the boy with his head down and butted him in the stomach. The victim was the taller of the two, so the blow landed in the right place, and before there was time to recover from it Anderson had seized the kitten; the others shouted with delight, for it did not occur to them that his sudden act was anything but a bid to be the executioner himself; but when the truth became clear to them and they saw their prey slipping from them, they made for Anderson whose practical mind was aware now that home was no longer a danger but a haven. He set off for it with the whole lot at his heels and the kitten, now the only creature that misunderstood his motives, clawed his hands.

It was unlucky for him that his road lay uphill and that he was rather blown from the violence of his onslaught, but the surprise it had created and the fact that his enemy had sat violently down among the feet of his companions delayed matters a little. They started after him, leaving their shaken leader to pick himself up. Anderson ran on, but a glance over his

H. Duthie

shoulder showed him he had no time to lose. He made all the speed he could but the hill was against him and, with blind instinct, he fled to a tree standing near; it was not big enough to be a protection but it was the one solid thing by the empty road; to the cat it was everything, for as he put his back to it and turned to face his pursuers the little beast sprung from his shoulder and clawed its way up into the lower branches.

"We'll hae't yet!" shouted a boy. But Anderson's face was not reassuring and one of the smaller ones began to cry.

The effect on the company was bad and they stood in a little malicious knot, turning the situation over in their minds. Anderson must be got the better of, but they did not know how to do it. The cat, high up among the boughs, looked down, round-eyed, as though it thought little of its champion's chances. Its mouth opened soundlessly, now and again, in a pink spot. The boys drew together, a mob in miniature.

"What'll ye gie's the poosie for?" cried one, coming a little forward—not far, but a pace or two, "ye'll get a sweetie frae wee Charlie's bag—or mebbe them a'."

Wee Charlie, to whom this juggling with other people's possessions was not pleasant, turned round and would have retreated, had he not been laid hold of.

"Wull ye gie's the poosie?" cried the other again.

"Na," said Anderson.

"But, we'll get it, aye wull we!"

There was a rush and two of them made a dive at him, but his Sunday boots were new and had thick soles. There was a howl of pain as the attackers fell back.

"Bide you, bide you yet and we'll sort ye!" cried a voice from the enemy's rear, "here's the stanes we've gotten for the poosie!"

One whizzed through the air and missed its mark, striking harmlessly against the tree trunk above Anderson's head. As others followed he ducked again and again and at last a shot caught him on the cheek and a little line of blood began to trickle down. He rubbed it off, rather shaken in spite of his valour, but he stood his ground though his heart began to beat harder and the tears were not far from his eyes. It was happy for him that the person he most admired in the world was taking a leisurely Sunday stroll through the fields which brought him at this moment within fifty yards of the conflict.

"Hey!" he shouted at the top of very powerful lungs, and Anderson saw Willie Keith, his father's horseman, throw his long leg over the gate.

The assailants fled as one man, leaving wee Charlie toiling in their wake with his sweetie bag and crying on them to stop.

"What's wrang, laddie?" enquired Keith, as Anderson, now less of a champion and more of a little boy with a fast swelling face, seized him by the sleeve.

"I wadna gie them the cat."

"The cat—what-like cat?"

Anderson pointed up into the tree from which the kitten was looking down upon the astonished horseman. As the story came out he dabbed the cut cheek with his brightly patterned handkerchief. The enemy had stopped his flight and was sending shouts of defiance from a safe distance.

"Rin awa' hame noo, ma mannie," said Keith, "and get a drappie water tae yer face."

"Will ye no gang after them and sort them, Wullie?"

"Fie, let them be—but I'm thinkin' ye'll get yer licks when ye win hame."

"I'm no carin'," replied Anderson.

"Sic a lad! Come awa' noo and I'll gang back wi' ye."

"But I'll no leave the poosie." His voice shook a little.

"It'll dae fine whaur it is."

"But they ken it's there an' they'll be back tae get it!" cried Anderson, desperately.

Willie Keith was a humane young man. He pushed back his cap and stood regarding the forlon little image. Anderson's hair hung down limp on his swollen face and the wet mud that the stones had spirted up as they landed round him had plastered his clothes; he certainly needed someone to speak for him.

"See now, Anderson," said Keith, "dinna greet. I'll awa' up an' get the cattie tae ye."

"I'm no greetin'," he replied, a large tear rolling down and trickling on his coat.

The horseman swung himself into the tree.

"Come awa' noo, I'm tae gang hame wi' ye," he said when he had returned to earth and delivered the kitten into Anderson's arms. "I'd no like ye tae get yer licks."

But Anderson paid little heed, for he had attained his end and that was what mattered to him. Physical consequences were a detail, in spite of everything.

They set off up the road, a strange contrast, for Willie Keith was something of a dandy on Sundays. The handkerchief he had applied to Anderson's dirty cheek was a silk one; he brushed bits of lichen off himself as they went. The boy hugged the cat and stepped out; the horse-man—that great man—would see him through, he believed, if there should be any question of parting him from his treasure. Much had been gained while the long lad strode at his side. All the same, as they neared the farm he was very silent. He knew that the large, slothful tabby which snored, day in, day out, by the kitchen range was the only animal allowed inside the house; the dog, when not on the chain, did not dare to violate the floors with its dirty footprints. He confided these anxieties to his companion as they went.

"Ye'll gie't tae me and I'll keep it," said the horseman as they parted at the farm gate.

"But ye'll no be tae droun it, Wullie?"

"Na, na. Ye're nae better nor a fule, Anderson, Awa ye gang. Ye'll hae it back the morn's morn."

It said much for the boy's belief in his friend that he handed him the cat without another word and went to meet his fate.

It was early next morning when the farmer went out and passed the bothie adjoining the farm buildings in which his horseman and the odd man had their habitation. Willie Keith was coming out of it with his coat over his arm.

"There's a terrible mice i' the stable," he said, solemnly.

"There's plenty traps about the place and ye ken whaur tae get them as weel as me," said the farmer, dryly. He was in a hurry and it was not like Keith to worry him about trifles.

"Aye, but they're that wise-like they winna gang in. Ye wadna credit the common sense o' thae brutes when they're aifter the oats."

"Tak' the cat frae the hoose," said the master.

"She's owre fond o' the fire. She wadna bide. We'd be the better o' anither ane."

"Get it then, an' dinna bother me."

"I've got it," said the horseman, pulling the kitten from under his coat.

"Lord sake, man, what's the use o' a thing that size?"

But Keith did nothing by halves.

"They're best young," he said, pontifically. "THEY LAIRN THE PLACE."

MacNichol looked at him to see if he was joking, but the young man's grave face told him nothing.

"But it's sic a helpless thing. Wha's tae gie't its meat? The mistress'll no thole it i' the hoose."

"I was thinkin' Anderson micht tak' it," said Keith, meditatively. "He's got sic a grand way wi' beasts."

"Weel, gie't him then an' awa' wi' ye!".

93

⟞ Business and Pleasure ⟝

Horace De Cardley gave his hat and coat to the parlourmaid and followed her into the room. He was a man of a little more than middle height and a little less than middle age; his hair lay smoothly brushed back from a colourless face and a stripe of braid ran down either trouser-leg. He was both noiseless and gentle. As he was announced, the woman who sat alone on the divan on the further side of the room came forward.

"This is very pleasant," said De Cardley, as he looked round when they had shaken hands.

He did not mean the room itself, because it was extraordinarily vulgar. The fire blazed high in the grate under a festooned drapery of Indian stuff which concealed the lines of the mantelpiece, and the furniture, but for the divan, was one riot of musharabiyah carving and Benares brass. On the right, near the fireplace, there was a door smothered in peacock blue curtain inlaid with little rounds of looking glass, and another door leading to the tiny dining-room of the flat was decorated in the same way. Where the walls were not draped they were plastered with framed photographs.

"This is not very like you," observed De Cardley, smiling as his eyes roved about.

"Indeed, no," said she. "I took it as it stands for three weeks."

"I really wonder you can endure even that."

"I shall not endure it much longer; I am leaving the day after to-morrow."

"And who are all these?" he asked, waving his hands towards the framed photographs.

"*Chi lo sà?*" said she.

De Cardley sat down, looking at Teresa Gordon with pleasure and interest. He had asked for an appointment "to talk business", and she had invited him to dine *tête-à-tête*. She had touched upon business with an airiness that did not match his own idea of the matter which was bringing them together. Most people will be stimulated by the sight of another person—one who just falls short of being an antagonist—lightly approaching a subject which they themselves know to be serious. Horace was no exception. He was entertained and pleased.

Teresa sat back with her light brown head outlined against the glaring cushions of the divan, contemplating him with calm eyes. Her long, very white neck was unornamented and her grey gown almost Puritanical; her widow's weeds had been put off some time before. She had not much reason for regretting Gordon and she was not a woman of pretences.

When dinner was announced he followed her into the dining room.

The round table was a gleam of whiteness and electric light made the bunch of lemon coloured chrysanthemums in the middle seem more immaculately chilly than anything De Cardley had seen for some time. Teresa Gordon looked as immaculate as they, but Horace reflected that she was hardly so chilly. What he carried in his breast pocket proved that. He ate his dinner with enjoyment and with an ironical appreciation of the complete unconcern that enveloped his companion.

"We will have coffee here," said she, as she pushed the silver cigarette-box towards him.

The coffee and the curls of smoke, the chrysanthemums, the sight of her long, white hand resting on the table caressed De Cardley's senses and loosened his self-conscious deliberateness from about him.

"We have a good deal to discuss, haven't we?" he began.

"Pleasure first and business after," said Teresa.

"As you like," replied he.

"Then we won't mix them."

"You know, you are a miracle of detachment," observed De Cardley.

Most of the women he knew were ready enough to discuss themselves; but she sat silent and he came within moderate distance of being ruffled.

"Why so impersonal?" he enquired.

"Pleasure before business, as I said. I can be personal in the other room."

At last, when the cigarettes were finished, Teresa rose and they went out.

"Please poke the fire," she said, as she sat down in her old place.

"Have I known you seven years, Mrs Gordon?"

"Not quite," she replied, with a little laugh, "but I will overlook that."

95

He stirred the coals to a blaze, laid down the poker and stood on the rug, drawing himself up.

"Now," said she, "—business. You begin, please. And remember it *is* business. From this moment I cease to be your hostess. I am merely an opposing or consenting opinion."

He laughed and then stared down at the polished toes of his shoes.

"Well," he began, raising his eyes to hers, "to start with, you told me that you did not believe I had got the letter—that I was bluffing, in fact."

She inclined her head.

"For that reason I have brought it," said De Cardley. "It is in my pocket."

"Then I owe you an apology and I now make it."

There was a pause.

"First, I will tell you *how* I got it."

"Will you really?" said she. "I should hardly think that would be pleasant."

He winced, ever so slightly.

"You wrote it early on the day of Gordon's death, if you remember," he went on.

"I remember," said she, a shade crossing her face.

"And when it was written, what did you do with it? I ask, because in fairness to myself, I must do so; for your answer may help to prove the rest of my words."

"I am quite willing to tell you," said Teresa. "I was going across the hall with the letter in my hand when the butler came running to tell me that the car was smashed to pieces and that they were bringing Gerald in. I forget what I did with it then, but I believe I flung it on the nearest table."

"Now I will take up the story," said De Cardley. "Not an hour afterwards, I was in the smoking room—you were upstairs—the house was all in confusion. I sat listening to the voices and footsteps and keeping myself out of the way. At last a footman came in with the afternoon post and a heap of letters was given to me in a lump on a tray."

"Ah—h," exclaimed Teresa, under her breath.

"I took up the lot in my hand without a thought and opened them, one after another, as I often do, without looking at the addresses; I had read one of them almost to the end before I saw that it was directed to another man. 'Ernest Lang, Esquire, Leopold's Drift, Rhodesia' was the address."

"I quite understand," said Teresa. "The incoming post must have been put down on the top of my letter. Everything was at sixes and sevens that day."

For a minute neither spoke.

"Well, to go on," said Teresa, at last. "I suppose you finished the letter."

"I did. There were only a couple or so of lines left to finish."

"It would have been a pity to miss the signature, wouldn't it?" said she.

"I had guessed that," replied De Cardley, with meaning.

"That is certainly one for you."

"I put it in my pocket; it was scarcely the kind of letter that you would care to be reminded of while Gerald was lying dead in the house. I knew—as everyone who had eyes and ears in their head must have known—what kind of a life you led with him, and that what had happened was nothing short of a release for you—that is true, Mrs Gordon—you know it is true."

"It is absolutely true," said she.

"But, at the same time, I did not suppose it would gratify you to be reminded that you had actually anticipated that release—that you had written to tell Lang that you were ready to come to him—that you had determined you could stand Gordon no more. It would be like paying accidentally for a thing that you were to have for nothing. Nobody likes that! So I kept the letter to myself. . . ."

"And why did you not return it to me later?"

"Well—I got a new train of ideas. I discovered that I did not want you to go to Lang; neither to marry him nor to—to do anything else. I did not know him; I had never seen him; but I was certain that when he saw Gordon's death in the newspapers—for the death of a man as well known as he was is not hidden under a bushel—he would write to you and between you you would soon find out that the letter had gone astray. Misunderstandings of that sort don't happen much outside melodramas, you know."

"Then I can't see what you proposed to yourself in keeping it back," she broke out.

"Wait. I have not done. I said to myself, 'now she is free, she may reconsider her intention, she may pick and choose. She may be passionately in love with Lang, or he may have stood to her as a refuge—a refuge to be counted on—an agreeable refuge, no doubt, but perhaps, no more.' And I told myself that there might be time for another man to step in. As you have since discovered, I had a mind to step in myself."

He paused, but she said nothing.

"It was only a chance, but I thought it might be worth trying for, and after a year, when I could hear of no sign of your starting life afresh, I wrote, but you had gone abroad and I could never find out where, though perhaps I can guess now."

97

"I was in Italy," said Teresa.

"Really?"

His intonation was odious.

"Well, anyhow you kept yourself very dark," he went on, "but you got tired of it in another ten months and came back. I saw you in the street and I wrote to you and you refused me."

"What could you expect?" exclaimed she. "I had never shown any special interest in you. You were a neighbour to whom I was willing to be civil, that's all. The fact that your people lived a couple of miles off brought us into contact and prevented our losing sight of one another."

"I prevented it too. I did not mean to be forgotten."

"I was a good deal astonished at your proposal."

"That is what all women say."

"It is what one woman says, who means it," replied she, roused. "I never trusted you and, to be frank, I never liked you."

"And *I* did not appreciate the tone of your letter when you answered me. You let your dislike appear so plainly that I thought it would be interesting to let you know what I could show you, if I chose. So I told you what had become of your letter to Lang. That brings us up to date, I think."

"And now," said Teresa, boldly, "you will give it back to me, which you should have done some time ago, and we will put the matter behind us."

He looked at her, the admiration that she compelled in him tempered with impatience; her audacity was splendid but she was carrying it too far.

"And what advantage should I expect from doing so?" He looked at her in a way that made the blood rise to her face.

"Oh, if it is of any importance to you, I shall think of you with a little less contempt than I do now. That is all."

"Absolutely all?"

"Mrs Gordon, you are cutting you own throat."

"Let us have done with this!" exclaimed she. "You seem unable to understand that I am not afraid of you!"

"Do you really think I should be such a fool as to give this up?" he asked, tapping his pocket.

"You appear to be quite astonished that I expect you to behave as a gentleman," replied she, "but perhaps you are right."

"You asked me here tonight to talk business," he said, "but I don't consider this *is* business. All I have gathered is that your dislike of me is even greater than I imagined."

"Dislike is a poor word," said Teresa, looking steadily at a point between his eyebrows, "but it will do. My first request is to be allowed to see that letter."

"I will read it aloud to you," said he, with malice.

She met him with perfect frankness. "I should dislike that too, I should prefer to read it myself."

"No doubt. But what guarantee have I that you won't toss it into the fire when you have got it? It would be a good chance of settling our business pleasantly."

"You can have my word that I will return it; I can offer you no more. But if you are anxious to read it, do."

He took it from his breast pocket and gave it to her. It was still in its envelope and she drew it out and went through it slowly.

"Yes," she said, "that is my handiwork. I remember writing every word of it. Thanks."

She held it out to him as he stood facing her. His fingers closed on it, and he stood smiling, holding it conspicuously, delicately, as one holds out a tit-bit "on trust" in front of some pet animal.

Teresa leant back, her hands crossed.

"You shall have it—at a price," he said.

"If you are wise," said she, "you will put it in the fire."

He had never before heard her say anything so futile and a sound of exasperation broke from his lips. As he would have turned from her in impatience he found his arms grasped, just above the elbows, in a grip that made him wince.

"Open your hand and drop that letter," said a voice behind him.

De Cardley would have faced about, but found it impossible. In the looking glass which hung over the mantelpiece beside him he saw his own reflection and that of a tall, clean-shaved man. The curtains over the front of the door near the fireplace were moving, as if someone had just passed between them.

He made another effort to free himself.

"Be good enough to let me go!" he exclaimed, angrily.

For answer, the man behind him pressed his thumb into a nerve just above De Cardley's funnybone and the letter dropped from his powerless fingers to the floor. He tried to put his foot upon it and received a backward jerk that threw him off his balance. He did not fall because the stranger held him up.

"Would you mind picking up that letter?" said the latter, speaking to Teresa. "I am sorry to have to ask you, but you see my hands are needed elsewhere."

She rose and took up the folded paper from the carpet.

"Put it in the drawer of that carved table and turn the key," said the man who was holding De Cardley. "I can get it afterwards."

When she had done so he let De Cardley go.

Horace was shaking with rage. He watched the tall man take the key from Teresa and slip it into his trouser pocket; the indignity of a struggle which he feared would be ineffectual was out of the question, a thing he dared not risk. He could only stand still with fury and mortification raging in his heart.

"I am sorry I was obliged to handle you so roughly," said the other man; "one does not like to do these things, but I had no choice."

The words were spoken quite simply, without the least trace of insolence, but they only maddened De Cardley the more. His antagonist had the clear greyness of eye that is seen in so many sailors, combined with a more sophisticated expression than the sea generally gives to the men who go down to it in ships. He was spare-looking, and rather younger than Horace.

The latter turned to Teresa as soon as he could command his voice.

"Perhaps you may find me as inconvenient without the letter as I was with it," said he, almost in a undertone; "you are not wise, Mrs Gordon, in spite of your bravado. It isn't exactly prudent to make an enemy of someone who finds you here alone in a flat with a man who appears to be as much at home in it as you are."

"I suppose you will tell all London," said Teresa.

The tall man was taking a cigarette from his case.

"You will hardly venture to deny that you are her lover?" sneered De Cardley, turning to him. "I shall not believe you if you do, and most certainly neither will anybody else."

"I shall not deny it," said the other.

De Cardley was dumbfounded, even shocked. He had never heard a woman given away so coldbloodedly before. Teresa Gordon was a cool hand but she seemed to have met her match in the man for whom she had thrown her reputation to the winds. He had already guessed at his identity.

"I shall wish you good night now," he said to Teresa, "and I may add that I think you are likely to repent you foolhardiness. You have treated me infamously—infamously! And I shall not forget it."

"Come, that's enough," said the other man. "I will let you out."

He moved to the door and De Cardley followed. The two stood in the hall. When Horace had put on his coat he turned to his companion.

"I can't think what the devil it is to you *who* has got that letter," he said. "You've done for Mrs Gordon, and if you're Lang, as of course you are—"

"But I'm not Lang," said the other. "Lang's dead, poor devil."

De Cardley stood stock still on the threshold, staring.

"Look in tomorrow's *Morning Post* and you'll see my name," said the tall man. "Mrs Gordon and I were married very quietly yesterday. Now go."

The Wade Monument

My uncle Frederick died in the early days of 1915, and so, though he left me his house, a little money and a good many miscellaneous possessions, it was only a few months ago that I was able to examine them or to have any idea of what the latter consisted. I was on the Western Front during the first half of the Great War, and when I recovered from the severe wound which brought me home and it was decreed that I could march no longer, I left the Service and went as an ambulance driver to Palestine. After the armistice I settled with my lame leg and a new-made wife in uncle Frederick's house, where I began, in time, to go through a very wilderness of boxes filled with his private papers.

I had always liked my uncle. He was a tall, spare man who looked like an American—that type of old-fashioned, rather grim American seen in illustrations to New England tales—clean shaven, in semi-clerical black. He always wore the strangely-shaped tall hat of his youth. Where he got these hats from I know not, but they must certainly have been made specially for him. He enjoyed what used to be called "an elegant leisure", living out his bachelor life among his books. He wrote voluminously; notes, extracts, comments; though these seemed to produce no result, in that they never saw the light. I used to suppose that they were the outcome of some definite system of thought, but when I came to look at the contents of the boxes, what struck me most was that no plan was distinguishable. He must simply have had a passion for recording. There were no consecutive diaries, nothing but records of things seen, things heard, things remembered. It was the sense of history run wild. What gave them value was the mellow humanity of the mind running through the patchwork.

It is one of these isolated papers that I now give in full, just as it came into my hands; carefully written and with the leisureliness that was in his speech and ways.

I had not long left Oxford in 1876 when I first went to Mintern Brevil. I cannot quite recall what took me there, but I think it was the talk of some casual acquaintance who drew an alluring picture of the quaintness of the small seaside towns on that line of coast stretching between Southampton and Plymouth. Perhaps it was hardly the neighbourhood that a young man, presumably athirst for life, might be expected to choose as a recreation ground; but out-of-the-way places have appealed to me always, and I think there is scarcely anything more interesting than to step quietly into some backwater and to let its history and suggestions gradually reveal themselves. It is like descending into an almost dark cave and waiting till the surrounding details come out of their obscurity and the slowly adjusting eye becomes aware of unsuspected objects, crannies, strange stones, footmarks in the sand. The obvious history of a place is accessible to all who desire to know it, but the other, shadowy history, which is the reality of the composite thing, which has brought its coherent parts together, which is, as the root of the flower, hidden in the ground—that is the soul of it all. I did not know this when I was a young man, or rather, I had not formulated the knowledge, but, looking back on myself, I can see that it influenced me.

It was June and I had taken a room in a farmhouse near the top of the steep hill that runs down to the town. The sea below was blue and glittering like a foreign sea and the houses were clustered in the little bay. That outburst of white flowers which comes with the near approach of midsummer was lighting up bank and hedgerow—white chervil, like lace, white catchfly, ox-eye daisies, and the white burnet rose—all were dazzling in the sunlight. Down the hill above the main part of the town, its western door almost in the street, its eastern wall on the cliff, stood the parish church with a square tower, grey against the expanse of blue as one looked down on it. The sea had encroached and eaten away much of the coast by Mintern Brevil, crawling up as though waiting at the foot of its crumbing ramparts to swallow church and churchyard in the fullness of time.

One evening, strolling by, I turned aside up the steps and entered the porch. The main body of the church looked attractive from the inside, being on a higher plane than the spot on which I stood and so giving a different general impression from that produced by the interior of ordinary places of worship. It appeared to be more old-fashioned than ancient and a gallery ran round three sides of the building, under which I passed as I emerged from the porch. There were many memorial tablets round the walls and a few large monuments with the usual urns and emblems. I never could resist memorial tablets. Their occasional bits of information and humanity challenge my mind to clothe the recorded names with personalities, and they raise a whole concourse of sailors lost at sea, soldiers fallen in half-forgotten campaigns, women long widowed, and pompous-sounding lawyers and divines. I have always found a few bare words of detail on a memorial tablet worth volumes anywhere else.

There was a tall marble slab on the wall of the northern aisle which bore an immense amount of lettering, and I went over to see whether there was anything suggestive to be found there. So long was it and so wordy that I had to sit down in a neighbouring pew to read it. It was a perfect example of those records of human hypocrisy which were the delight of the early nineteenth century, and it commemorated a family belonging to the town. I wondered if there were any descendants left alive to be put to the blush every Sunday by its weary and fulsome pomp. Were there *any* to whom the following could commend itself? . . .

Sacred to the memory of
THOMAS CORBY WADE, Esquire, Solicitor,
Born at Mintern Brevil, February 24th, 1780.

An affectionate Father and devoted Husband, he fulfilled his private Duties in the same Christian Spirit which actuated his every Public Deed. His strict and honourable probity was the pride of his Fellow Townsmen. His Charities were munificent. To an Upright Character he joined a Suavity of Address which gained him the consideration of all who came in contact with him in his Daily Walk of Life. He contributed largely to every Municipal Scheme which his Enlightened Judgement approved and was untiring in his efforts to ameliorate the condition of the Deserving Poor. He died, the True Example of a Professing and Believing Christian, at his Residence in Avon Street, Oct. 1st, 1841, aged 61 years, regretted by an Afflicted Family and an Inconsolable Public.

Also of

His wife, ELIZA, daughter of the Rev. W. CLARK, Vicar of Cobton, in the country of Dorset. Born June 5th 1796. Died Aug. 19th, 1835, aged 38 years. A tender wife and mother, bringing up her children in the fear of the Lord and providing a pattern for her neighbours of all that a pious Christian woman should be.

Also of

THOMAS CLARK WADE, M.D., son of the above, whose brilliant intellectual gifts earned universal acclamation and whose practice was one of the largest in the south-west of England. Born March 23rd, 1815. Died esteemed and in full assurance of salvation, May 3rd, 1858, at the age of 43.

Also of

MARY ELIZA. Born Oct. 12th, 1817, who died in Infancy.

Also of

EDWIN, born Dec. 1st, 1818, who by his industry and talents made a large fortune in Jamaica, and died 1858, in pious resignation to his Maker's will, from the results of an accident. Lamented by all who had the privilage of knowing him.

Then came a gap, and some way further down the stone were these words:

Alured. Died 1851.

I rose, exasperated. I could picture this intolerable family, whose only recommendation in my eyes was the fact that almost all its members had died moderately young. I looked with relief on a small brass not far off which bore merely the name and age of an obscure officer who had ended his life on the Gold Coast, dying of yellow fever in the place to which his duty had taken him. What a happy contrast to the tame brood of Wades with their resounding complacent virtues! The only original thing about the Wade monument was the odd contrast between "Alured" and his relations, for his name stood apart from theirs as though unfit to appear in that galaxy of rectitude. Why was he so slighted? Why was there not so much as a word to give him significance in that welter of words? I wondered whether he had "died in infancy", like "Mary Eliza", but the time elapsed between his mother's death and his own forbade the possibility.

I made my way to the western gallery. It was Jacobean, of fine carved wood, and having examined it from below I ran hurriedly up the stairs, for the light was failing and there was a piece of tapestry on the wall behind the gallery pews that I was curious about. One does not often find tapestry in churches.

I paused for a moment in the front seat. From that position I could see the Wade monument, and I was astonished to notice that a woman was sitting just where I had sat to examine it and was doing the same thing. I

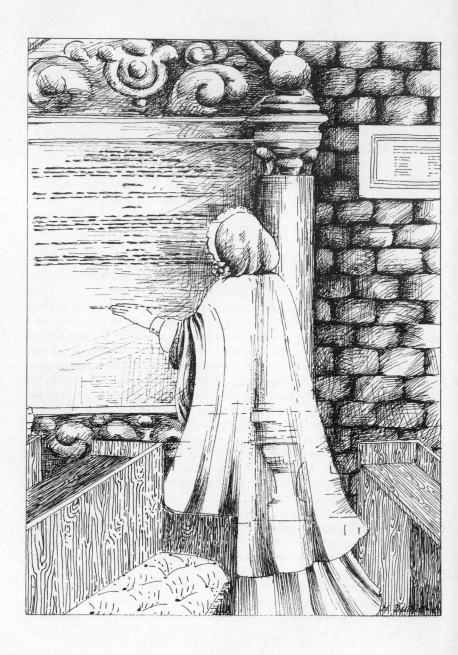

was puzzled because I had come up the short stair in a couple of bounds and was certain that the pew was empty when I put my foot on the first step. To reach that spot before I could look down she must have run.

She was a small person, and though I could only see her back, I could guess that she was in distress, for she sat with her head bent forward, and now and again I saw her put her hand up to her eyes. I quite forgot the tapestry in looking at her. She wore a sort of grey cape trimmed with blue; though I did not know much about the fashion of woman's garments I could see that she was dressed like no one I had ever met. All at once she rose and crossed the aisle, showing a small-featured profile and the frilled grey border of the hood or cap she wore. There was something blue on it, too—a rosette or a lappet, or whatever these things are called. To my further astonishment she went up to the Wade monument and stood in front of it; then she put out her hand, and there was just enough light left for me to see that she passed it over a part of the stone with a movement that was almost a caress.

I sat rigid, afraid lest the least sound should disturb her. She went back to her place in the pew, and sank down on her knees, and I knew by her heaving shoulders that she wept, but so silently that not a sob woke the quiet of the empty church—empty but for myself sitting breathless in the gallery. Then she rose and crossed to the centre aisle, without looking up, and passed out by the main door just below the place where I sat.

It was on a Monday that I saw her, and she was a good deal in my mind during the week. Once I thought I had caught her figure disappearing down a side street of Mintern Brevil; once I had a fancied glimpse of her grey cap behind the curtain of a window, though I could not be sure; but when Sunday came I went to the parish church—purposely, not too early—that I might peep throught the door at the worshippers in the north aisle. If the seat in which we had both sat were her own, and were she there, I might contrive to get a place near enough to it to see her. I wondered at the time why I was impelled to take so much trouble; I think I am less surprised now.

Prayers had began as I stood at the door to peer in, and waiting till the congregation rose from its knees, I had full opportunity for my search. There she was, in the same pew at the end next the aisle, with her grey and blue tippet, sitting upright this time, as though oblivious of all that was going on, quite still. As the Amen produced a general movement, I saw that a verger was observing me from beyond the Wade monument and I stepped quickly forward to get nearer to my goal before he should

107

be upon me to regulate my movements. We met exactly parallel to it, and he took me by the arm.

"Two vacant seats there," he said, thrusting me towards the pew in which the lady sat.

We were close beside her, and she looked round at me, making no movement to let me pass in. I hesitated.

"Two vacant seats, sir," repeated the verger, more loudly.

There was only one that I could see, on the other side of the quiet little figure; I was shocked at the man's free and easy manner, for he leaned across her, pointing, stretching his arm just in front of her face. It seemed all the worse to me because I had begun to suspect the odd little woman of not being in her right mind, and I was angry to think that he should so take advantage of her weakness. I made a sort of apologetic bow, and went in, because it seemed the only way to put an end to his impertinence, and because the further occupants of the pew were looking at us intently.

There was a hassock in front of her and her feet were on it. As she did not stir them I stepped over, and, being nervously anxious not to incommode her, laid hold of the ledge where the prayer-books lay to steady myself, and in so doing dropped my stick.

It fell against her knees, but, instead of sliding down the slope of her skirt, passed straight through it to the floor, as a stone might fall through transparent water. I could see it lying upon the boards, although the grey folds of her dress and the outline of her limbs were between me and it.

I subsided into my place, staggered beyond all power of expression. For some time I was too much bewildered to notice the looks of surprise and censure cast on me by those who stood beyond us; I merely sat on, *though all were standing, and the Jubilate* was ended and the psalms begun before I had the sense to rise to my feet. I took up a prayer-book mechanically and turned over the leaves, unable to concentrate my mind on finding the place. My right-hand neighbour pointed it out with a detached disapproval of manner that would have annoyed me had I been capable of feeling anything. I was in the mental condition of a man who has suddenly fallen into the sea and been as suddenly pulled out, who lies on the beach unable to adjust himself to a dry and stationary world. When I had recovered a little I glanced stealthily at the woman on my left, but she appeared to be as solid as anybody else. She inspired no dread in me. My only trouble was the difficulty of keeping my head in her presence. I was young, and therefore acutely conscious of the attitude of strangers towards me, and I greatly feared to make myself ridiculous.

In time I grew more calm and began to argue with myself. I did not dream—I knew that I was sober and I believed that I was sane; I hardly dared to look directly at her, though I much wished she would turn her head and let me see whether there were traces of the distress of a few days ago. No one else appeared to be interested in her. I wondered why the verger had been so boorish—surely if she frequented the church he would have known her and hesitated to treat her so rudely, lest he should be taken to task by some looker-on who knew her too. Then I recalled his words: "*Two* vacant seats, sir", and the truth broke on me.

He had not seen her. Presumably it was I, and I only, who was aware of her presence.

I became more and more convinced that this was a fact. Though I could see no difference between the solidity of her face and that of the faces near us, her feet and the lower part of her skirt now seemed hazy to my eyes, shadows beneath which lay the walking-stick I had not dared to recover. My own figure hid them from the people beside me. All that had disturbed these latter was my apparently futile agitation and the clumsiness of my entrance.

It was not until the sermon that my strange neighbour turned towards me, and, looking at me with the appealing gaze of a dumb creature, lifted her arm and pointed to the Wade monument. I made the slightest movement of assent, afraid to give myself prominence, yet unable to resist the troubled eyes. Her act finally confirmed my belief, because, though she had stretched out her arm over the end of the pew, no one had shown a sign of astonishment. She looked middle-aged, not from any lines traced by the years, but from the frilled cap she wore and the prim fashion of her clothes. The eyes that met mine were clear, rather childish, though set in a woman's face and full of a dumb anxiety that was very pitiful. I raised my brows as if to ask a question and waited, wondering if she would understand. She nodded, pointing to an open hymn-book lying before me. I slid it along the ledge to her, but she shook her head and signed to me that I should lay it upon my knee. When I had done this she drew close to me, so close that the end of her tippet lay across my cuff; though I felt no touch, no warmth from the face so near my own as she took a gold-headed pin from the fastening of her dress and indicated letters, one after another, in the printed page. Then she paused, scanning my face, whilst I read the word they formed. It was A-l-u-r-e-d.

It is almost impossible to describe the state of mind into which those three syllables threw me. To say that I was bewildered is to say nothing; but the sense of something compelling and inevitable—of having known all the time in some recess of my being that I was concerned with the name of this man—was so strong that self-consciousness fled and I forgot everybody in the church but the one who, so to speak, was not there. I took out my pocket-book and wrote down the six letters whilst the anxious eyes near my shoulder followed every line. The gold-headed pin was still till my pencil should stop. Then, when I looked round for further guidance, the face and the tippeted figure had faded into nothingness and only the pin was visible against the page of the hymn-book, pointing to the letters which followed. A-v-o-n S-t-r-e-e-t s-e-a-r-c-h. I had just time to write them when it ceased and was gone.

Through the rest of the sermon I sat without hearing a word. The place beside me was empty, and I was left with a maddening curiousity and the fear lest I should never be able to gratify it. I put away my pocket-book.

As I walked home I decided that I would not look at it again till next day. "If this is really an illusion," I said to myself, "I shall find to-morrow that there is nothing written here."

I went out into the fields that afternoon, and, lying under a clump of bushes, turned the experience of the morning over and over. There was trouble about this man, Alured, though he was dead; that was plain enough, and I began to piece together the scraps that had been committed to me and to compare them with what I could recall of the words on the monument. "Avon Street" was suggestive, for the inscription said that Alured's father had died at "his residence" there. It was there evidently, that "search" should be made. I wondered whether the house was still standing. There was nothing to be done to-day, Sunday, for all the shops were closed and I had no acquaintance from whom I could seek information. True, there was my landlady; but when I made inquiry of her that evening it profited me nothing, for I was confronted with that dreadful obstacle, the blank wall of the purely domestic mind.

Next day I went down to Mintern Brevil. One subject had driven all others from my mind. I had lain awake half the night. My idea was to question the tradesmen and innkeepers, to tap that stream of gossip and reminiscence which flows under the life of all small towns. I did not know Avon Street, but I was curious to see the "residence" of the Wades; it was no detective spirit which urged me, but my own sense of romance—strong in those days—and the fantastic hope of doing some possible service, palliating some undiscovered grief. I do not think I was a superstitious young man, and had I been so, superstition could hardly be said to enter into the case. I was not concerned with superstition, one way or another. I had merely seen a strange thing, as I might have seen an elopement or a street accident, and I wanted to know all that might be known about it. It seemed no part of my duty to persuade myself that it had not happened.

I had just passed the church when I cursed myself for a fool. Why not go in? Why not go back to the same place? Why not take up the hymn-book and see whether the anxious figure would appear at my side and join again the thread which had broken so quickly? The door was open, the place empty, and in I went.

I sat down and took up the book, and to make the parallel complete, sought for the same place in it. I had forgotten the page and had to turn up the first line of the hymn in the index. When I had done so I looked up and saw the little woman standing beside the Wade monument. I cannot say I *saw* her come towards me, for the next thing I was aware of was her presence at my side and her hand holding the gold-headed pin.

This time I was less taken aback and more able to think for myself, so I brought out my pocket-book and, laying it beside the other on my knee, I wrote "which house?" after the "Avon Street" I had already traced there.

The pin moved as it had done before.

"A t-r-e-e."

"Am I to search the tree?" I wrote.

"S-e-a-r-c-h t-h-e l-a-d-d-e-r - r-o-o-m d-o t-h-i-s f-o-r A-l-u-r-e-d."

"I will," I wrote; but I broke off, for the pin was running on again.

"B-e-h-i-n-d t-h-e d-i-a-m-o-n-d-s f-o-r p-i-t-y-s s-a-k-e f-o-r p-o-o-r A-l-u-r-e-d."

"But what am I to look for?"

As I wrote this question—the crux of all—and waited for the expected answer, the pin was gone.

I left the church and went straight to Avon Street, directed by a passing workman, and embarked on the preliminaries of a search for something the very nature of which I did not know. I had written "I will" on the impulse of the moment, but I felt bound at least to try to make good my word. It might be an awkward task, but it was too late to think of that, for, wild goose chase or no, I was committed to it.

Avon Street was a quiet, remote place, not properly a street at all, but a row of detached houses far back from the sea and approached by a modest alley from the main thoroughfare. Only one true seaside touch

111

had cropped up in two or three of these, and that was the faded-looking green verandah with a sloping tin roof which seems to belong particularly to the south coast of England. Each had a small patch of garden railed in from the pavement, and I saw with interest that there was but one tree in the place, a large araucaria, luxuriantly grown, whose thin sombre arms shadowed the dead-looking windows by the door of the most old-fashioned of all. I had so far returned to a normal frame of mind that I smiled to think of my question of whether I should search the tree. I could not imagine how anyone would proceed who had to search a "monkey-puzzle".

If this house was the Wade house there would seem to be real meaning in the directions of the woman in the church, and I opened the iron gate and approached the door; I was not prepared to confront any remaining member of the family who might be within and to state my extraordinary errand, so I had no choice but to ask for a fictitious person and to hope that the act might elicit the name of the owner.

"Is Mr Jerningham at home?" I inquired, taking the first moderately uncommon name I could think of.

The thin-lipped woman who answered the bell eyed me resentfully.

"This is Miss Wade's house," she said, "we have no gentleman here."

She watched me departing, unmollified by my apology. I could feel her eyes on my back as I unlatched the iron gate.

It had been an easy thing to identify the "residence", but the next step—to get into it—would be a very different matter, and I felt a good deal discouraged. The keeper of the door seemed to look on me as an imposter (she little knew with what reason), and I could imagine that the dweller behind it, were I ever to reach her presence with my story, would take me for some wandering madman. A spinster—a member of the family described on the monument—what hope had I of being listened to by such a person! I went down to the shore and sat on the seawall to take council with myself what my next step should be.

I did not know much about the clergy. My father was at the bar and had no clerical friends. But when I came to consider which individual in a community would be most accessible to a stranger, I could only think of the parson. The longing to halve the burden of my experience was great, and I also reflected that, their family monument being set up in the parish church, the surviving Wades would probably belong to its congregation. I had not the vaguest remembrance of the last Sunday's preacher, for I had had other things to think of. However, I could come to no better conclusion and I made up my mind to appeal to him. But I would put it off till to-morrow; it would take me till then to screw up my courage.

Next day, cold with the dread of making a fool of myself to no purpose, I was ushered into the vicarage study where a pale, plain-looking little man rose to receive me. There was nothing remarkable about him but a crooked smile that gave character to his face. He asked me very civilly what he could do for me.

The knowledge of my position engulfed me as a wave engulfs a pebble on the shore. I was tongue-tied. Everything in the room was solid and spoke so loudly to settled habits, of daily duties, and all reasonable and accepted things that, in my acute consciousness of the fantastic nature of what I had come to say, my heart died within me. Here was the recognised exponent of spiritual things and here was I with this moonshine tale of the unseen upon my lips. I felt like a child with a tin sword before a general.

He was misled by my bearing, for it was plain that he suspected some young man's scrape, some difficulty which youth might sooner disclose to a stranger than to a parent. He gave me a little time to collect myself and then said with his crooked smile:

"You need not hesitate to tell me anything. What am I here for but to listen? If you speak plainly to me I will speak plainly to you—that is all."

So I began. I told it to him baldly and consecutively, from the beginning, when I stood idly before the Wade monument, to the end, when I turned my back on the house with the araucaria.

When I had finished he got up and stood by the mantel-piece.

"And this is *absolutely* true?" he said at last; "upon your honour, this is true?"

"Sir," I exclaimed, "can you suppose that I should put myself in this position for a childish invention? The risk of being taken for a liar is no advantage."

"I beg your pardon," said he.

"It is true, upon my honour."

He sat down again and we were both silent for a little while.

"What do you make of it, sir?" I inquired at last.

"I don't know what to make of it."

"And what ought I to do?"

He was looking at the floor and he raised his eyes to mine.

"You said you wrote 'I will', did you not, when she told you to search?"

"Yes."

"Then you must do it."

113

"You think there is something in it, then?" I exclaimed, catching at his support.

"I tell you I don't know what to think; but I am certain that we should keep our promises."

I nodded.

"Do you know anything of the family?" I asked; "I came here, hoping you might give me some help in finding them."

"Miss Emily Wade is the last one left now," he replied, "but though she is my parishioner, I can hardly say that I know her. The one I *can* tell you about is Alured Wade, though he has been dead these five and twenty years. It is owing to him that they left Mintern Brevil. The house was let at one time, but afterwards it stood empty till Miss Wade came back a couple of years ago. She sees nobody and goes nowhere, not even to church."

"But why is it owing to Alured?" I broke in.

"He was in a solicitor's office, and he made away with a large sum of money and died in prison. That is why they left the town and why she lives as she does. She had brought Alured up, for she was ten years older than he when they were left motherless. He died at twenty, poor wretched lad. I have only been here a few years, so I never saw him."

"There was something about diamonds too," said I. "It is written down in my pocket-book."

"I can't imagine what that can be. I have never heard anything about that."

"Well," said I, ruefully, "I must do my best, as you say, but how to approach Miss Wade I don't know, for it seems she is even more unapproachable than I suspected. If I write to her is there any chance that she will consent to see me? Is it too much to ask you to give me a word of introduction; I am really no impostor, but you do not know how I dread it."

"You are no coward, young man, all the same."

"I will try not to be," said I.

"Well," he went on, "you have no right to hang back, neither have I. I will go to Miss Wade, not because I think I can influence her to listen to you, but because she may think it less of an intrusion from one of my calling than from any other man. Go home now and wait till you hear from me."

I got up.

"I can never thank you enough, sir," I said.

"Wait to thank me till we have succeeded," he replied, smiling crookedly.

For two days after this conversation I dreaded the postman. I did not know which would make me more uncomfortable, a summons to Avon Street or the news that nothing further could be done; but on the third day I received a letter from the parson.

... I have had a difficult business [he wrote] and for some time I had little hope of success, but as last I have got Miss Wade's consent to see you and now I can only leave you to do your best. I told you that you were no coward, but I now add that you may possibly become one when you meet Miss Wade. Do not take this as discouragement, but as warning, and remember, if I may venture to advise you, that there is nothing like keeping one's temper in all circumstances. I hope you will let me hear whether any new light is thrown on this strange subject. . . .

*   *   *

At an appointed hour I stood once more on the threshold of the house with the araucaria, and this time was grudgingly admitted and taken across a small, dingy hall to a sitting-room on the ground floor. There was no one in it, and I had been waiting fully ten minutes when Miss Emily Wade entered.

I had no nerve consciously to observe the woman herself, but only to feel the effect she produced on me; though now, after the lapse of years, I can describe her in detail. At a little distance she appeared to be the embodiment of commonplace middle age, but as she advanced with a stiff bow, which was the mere drawing-in of her chin, and desired me to be seated, I saw my mistake. She was slow and cumbrous and her large face, almost pear-shaped, sallow and very smooth in its outlines, reminded me of something Asiatic. Though she was so large, you would not call her fat, for the softness suggested by that word was absent. She had the heavy thickness of something stuffed tightly with sawdust, and she wore a muslin cap with a velvet bow, the recognised head-dress of all well-to-do elderly women at that date. Her hair, showing no thread of grey, was parted smoothly. I think she had the smallest mouth I ever saw and the depth of her chin made it look as though set too high in her face. Her straight, heavy nose seemed to start too soon from between her brows. I have never known the colour of her eyes, for their opaqueness was all that I could realise. She sat down without a word and waited for

115

me to begin. There was not enough expression in her face to show hostility, but I felt it emanating from her.

How I embarked on my story I cannot remember. I heard myself speaking as though I were listening to another person, and the opaque, secretive eyes never left my face. I will do her the justice to say that she did not once try to interrupt me. When I had finished, a sense of ineptness and anticlimax and futility enfolded me like a choking mist.

"And why have you brought me this tale?" she inquired, a sneer touching her lip.

"I considered myself bound to do so."

"Indeed," she said, slowly, "and what do you expect to gain by it?"

"A clear conscience."

She looked disconcerted, I suppose, by the directness of my answer. It was the first indication of any kind of feeling that I had seen since she entered.

I do not know what happy intuition spurred me to thrust her up against the matter in question before she had recovered her balance, Her strength was to sit still and so, no doubt, instinct impelled me to keep her moving.

"I see that I have put you into an awkward position," I said.

"Not in the least, I assure you!" she exclaimed, a slight flush rising to her forehead.

It was evident to me that the very thought of herself in such a plight was intolerable to her.

"I am truly sorry to have upset you," I continued, "but I can well imagine that my intrusion is annoying. I——"

"You misunderstand me," she broke in. "I am entirely indifferent. Be sure of that."

"But it is very natural. Believe me, I have every sympathy with you, and I can only apologise, placed as I am. Perhaps you would like me to go?"

I half rose from my seat. It was a rash thing to do, for had she said "Yes" I should have had no choice but to depart. Despite the parson's advice I had let my irritation get the better of me in an overwhelming desire to shake her sullen insolence and the vanity which made her see herself as unassailable, imperturbable at all points. It was something inert and unenterprising in her that alone prevented her from dismissing a person who shook, even for a moment, her placid experience. Effort was her horror. I could guess that.

I think she would willingly have strangled me. Stupid though I believe she was, she had an uneasy feeling that I had made it difficult for her to dismiss me with dignity.

But her temper was suffering, as well as mine.

"I told the Vicar that I would see you and hear your—your—what you wanted to say—and I have done it. What do you want? Let us get through with it quickly," she exclaimed, angrily.

"Will you allow me to see the ladder-room, if there is such a place?" I asked, my own anger cooling as the prospect bettered itself.

"It is empty. There is nothing there."

"Then there *is* a room called the ladder-room! Let your maid take me there. I will not ask you to go with me."

"I will certainly go with you," she replied.

It was no civility which prompted her words; her look made their meaning plain. It said, "Do you suppose I should trust you out of my sight?"

But the desire to be disagreeable had betrayed her; it had gained me my point. She rose, and I opened the door and followed her out.

We went slowly up the dark stairs of the musty little house; it had three storeys and at each landing she stopped, breathing heavily, that I might understand the infinite inconvenience I was causing her. This made me very uncomfortable as a man. As a human being I cared nothing.

When we reached the top floor I found myself facing a ladder of about four rungs with a handrail at one side; it led to a door which looked as if it had not been painted for half a century.

"Go on," said Miss Wade.

I went up and thrust the door open; it needed a strong push and I almost stumbled into a small attic room, papered and with a dormer window in the sloping roof letting in the afternoon light. My companion came heavily after me. It was perfectly empty, but for three objects: a deal table in the recess of the window, a tiny, dusty picture hanging on a nail, and an unused bookshelf fastened on the wall. There was not so much as a fireplace.

Miss Wade stood looking at me with sullen triumph in her opaque eyes. Her mouth was pinched to a small line above the long bulk of her chin. I felt very foolish.

"And was this always known as the ladder-room?" I asked.

She assented.

In spite of the fact that the gold-headed pin had, so far, pointed to nothing but the truth, I could only stare round on the unpromising

117

place, humiliated by the ineffectual figure I cut. There was not even a drawer in the table that I might open. I went to the wall and peered at the little faintly-coloured daguerreotype in its frame that seemed cut out of black tin.

Then I started back and turned to Miss Wade. I suppose that triumph must have loosened her tongue, for the first words she had yet volunteered came from her pursed lips.

"My mother," she said, shortly.

I should have known the portrait, even without the grey cap and the tippet with blue trimming.

"That is the lady I saw in the church," I said.

I could not bring myself to ask Miss Wade whether this wretched attic had been Alured's room, but I felt sure of it. I did not know if she had learned from the Vicar that he had told me the boy's history and, in any case, I did not want to hear his name on her lips. The sight of the daguerrotype stirred an overwhelming pity in me. That was Alured's mother, the mother who had been replaced, for him, by the heavy, sordid woman in the doorway; I could imagine what such a change must have meant to the little boy who had slept in this fireless room. He had been "brought up" by her, been completely in her power; she had dealt out his punishments and held him, as grown-up people hold children, in the hollow of her hand. Here he had lived, the only young thing in the house, through his motherless years, only to die in prison at last. I thought of the desolating tears of my own happy childhood—rare, indeed, with me, but, probably, not rare with him. I could see him here, alone with his griefs and misunderstandings and hidden disappointments, under the attic roof, perhaps looking at the daguerreotype through wet eyelashes and knowing that his sins and fears and all the thousand, thousand childish secrets and dreads must be locked into his lonely heart because the face in the frame was only a face in a frame, and no more, I longed to be out of the house, anywhere away from Miss Wade. She was immeasurably more hateful to me now that I had seen this picture in this place.

"There are no diamonds here, after all, you see," she said.

As she spoke my eyes were on the bookcase. Perhaps, if she had not made that derisive speech, we should have left the miserable room no wiser than we came, but at the word "diamonds" I sprang forward, for light flashed into my mind. On the wall behind the empty bookshelves a piece of chintz was nailed to keep the books from rubbing it; it was a hideous thing, grimy and faded; blue, with a yellow diamond pattern covering its dismal expanse.

"Yes, there are," I cried, laying my palm against it. *"These* are the diamonds!"

There was a rent in the stuff where it was crossed by the middle shelf, but I could not get my hand into it because the horizontal board was set in so close to the wall. At the lower edge to the chintz a row of nails stretched it tight, and just above these I could feel a thin, square object lying as though in a pocket. Without further ado I got my thumb in between two of the nails and ripped up the rotten stuff. It tore at a touch and a slim paper packet fell out and dropped on the floor.

Miss Wade said nothing; anger and surprise devoured her. I could tell that her wrath was raised, not by my summary dealing with her furniture, but by the proof, now lying at my feet, that there had really been something to find and that I had found it. I picked up the packet and handed it to her.

"Thanks," she said, putting it into her pocket. "Now we will go downstairs."

Although there was the handrail, she had to turn and step backwards down the ladder. At any other time I should have laughed inwardly at the mixture of displeasure and physical discomfort on the large, white face. But I did not laugh now. I had reached the goal towards which my whole mind had strained for nearly a week; I had started on such a strange quest as few had ever undertaken; and now, what I suspected was the key of it all had passed into the hands of this repellent creature! In my folly I had not foreseen this very obvious climax, but I now saw it written on the pursed-up mouth and secretive eyes that would not meet my own. *I should hear nothing more;* I could not protest; I could do nothing but submit. She had turned the tables on me after all.

She stopped in the hall outside the sitting-room door, her hand on the door-knob, and made the same stiff bow with which she had received me. There was nothing for it but to take up my hat and go.

I was furious as I went up the street, outraged in every feeling. The consistent rudeness I had met with made my blood boil. Being very young, I marvelled that, in a civilised world, the attempt to do what was right—at some cost to myself, too—should bring me nothing but malice; and beyond that, baffled curiosity wept lamentably in my breast. It was cruel, abominable, that I should be debarred from knowing whether my thankless labours had been of any use to anyone, alive or dead.

*   *   *

I had lost all interest in Mintern Brevil. I was not such a fool as to imagine that Miss Wade would send me any information, and it seemed that the best thing I could do was to depart next day and try to forget the whole business. While I was packing, the Vicar walked up to the farm and asked me to spend a few days with him. I was immensely flattered, for I liked him, and shouldering my small portmanteau I accompanied him home.

We were at breakfast on the following morning when the post came in. I had no correspondence, but he had a good deal, and, when he had turned over his pile of letters, he opened one and became so much absorbed in it that he stopped eating. I went on steadily. At last he looked up.

"This is your affair, too," he said.

There had been three enclosures in the envelope and he threw one of them across to me.

Dear Mr. Williams [I read], The person you spoke of to me called at my house the day before yesterday and insisted upon my climbing with him to the attic. While we were there a packet dropped from behind a bookshelf. I think the information which it contained should be made public, and as I do not want to be annoyed by inquisitive people, I will ask you to do so by mentioning it, when opportunity occurs, to your parishioners. In order that you may speak with authority I enclose two letters which I shall be obliged if you will return. Meanwhile, I will consider what other steps should be taken.

Yours truly,
Emily Wade

"And now read this," said the Vicar, after I had finished. I took the yellow discoloured paper and smoothed it out.

October 12, 1850.

Dear Ned,—I have not had a moment's ease since our conversation after we left the office yesterday, for I can think of nothing but the terrible story you told me. You know what I feel. My friendship for you must give you full assurance of that, and the remorse you expressed as we walked home together will not be aggravated by any reproach from me. What is weighing on you is weighing on me too. Think of your mother lying there; we know from the doctor that she has only months to live—if that. What will it be to her? I am convinced, *determined*, that nothing must be left undone to spare her the knowledge that would prevent her from dying in

120

peace. This is my proposal, the plan I have thought out. I am going to take the theft upon myself. We must leave the matter alone till it is discovered; that will gain time, possibly much time, and I will then confess it, holding you bound to be silent. Ned, think of your mother. Remember that I am tied by none of the considerations that tie you. My father is dead ten years ago, my mother I can only vaguely remember; all I know of her is the picture in my room. My elder brothers are prosperous men who can take care of themselves. You know my sister. You, who have known me since we were both children, will understand what I need not say. Your mother's goodness and love to me when I most needed it is all I am thinking of now. I am not thinking of you. I am thinking of her. It is Sunday and my sister is at church, so I have had leisure to consider, and my mind is made up.

If you agree, *as you must do*, I will require you to do two things. You must write me a letter accepting the proposal I have made and giving me your word that as soon as your mother is dead you will acknowledge the truth. I will make a copy of this letter that I am now writing and seal it up with yours in a packet. It will be put in a place that only you and I will know of, and as soon as possible after your mother's funeral, you will carry it to a person whom we shall both select and who will know how to use it for my release.

We do not know how soon the discovery of what you have done may be made, so whatever we settle must be settled at once in all its details. I shall see you to-morrow at the office and we must walk home together. But before we meet I must tell you again, lest you should have any hesitation in agreeing, that *I am doing it for her.*

Your sincere friend,
Alured Wade

The Vicar pushed the other paper towards me. It was dated two days after the foregoing letter. The writer had not taken long in making up his mind.

I accept all the conditions of Alured Wade's letter of Oct. 12, 1850 [it ran], and I hereby faithfully promise that, on my mother's decease, I will do as desired by him with the two letters, using every endeavour to clear his name by means of them and by admitting the fraud which I have committed and for which he, for the reasons he states, has taken the blame.

Edward Groves Stephenson

"Poor lad," said the Vicar, "poor little lad."

His words took me back to the attic room with the little boy I had pictured alone in it. I was glad, more glad than I could say, to know that someone had befriended him; the measure of his gratitude showed me, like lamplight, how dark the dark places must have been to him. How glad I was that I had bearded that heavy woman with the oqaque eyes and the velvet bow in her cap! It rather awed me to think that I had been the means of disinterring that obscure and unrecognised sacrifice. For the moment I had forgotten the woman in the church, but she returned to my mind, bringing with her a mist of speculation in which I lost myself.

The Vicar's voice broke through it.

"There is another piece that fits into the story," he said. "I know the name of Ned Stephenson well. He disappeared very suddenly from Mintern Brevil, years before I came here; it was supposed, to America. In any case he was never heard of again. I wonder did his mother cheat the doctor and outlive Alured, and was his baseness a crime against his fellow-clerk, or against his fellow-clerk's memory? Did he break his word to a dead man or to a live one? There is nothing on the monument to tell how far into 1851 Alured lived; but he must have died without speaking."

"And I wonder," said I, "whether the packet fell down behind the chintz and was lost, or whether it was hidden there purposely till the time should come to produce it?"

"It must have been hidden," said he, reflectively. "If Alured had lost it, he would certainly have written another letter and made Ned write another statement, and if Ned had lost it, it would hardly have been found in the Wades' house. Had the real culprit made any attempt to tell the truth I should have heard of it when I first heard the story of Alured's crime. It is easy to guess why he disappeared."

"And the woman in the church?"

"We know nothing about anything," said he, "and I suppose Solomon himself was in the like position. But he said some notable things, all the same—'Many waters cannot quench love, neither can the floods drown it.' "

"Do you imagine that Miss Wade will add anything to the monument?" I asked, after a pause. "She ought to do him that much justice."

"Ah," he said, "I fancy that, whatever she does, her resentment will never be disturbed by a little thing like the truth. He brought discredit on her and she will never forgive him, as she will never forgive you for bringing back the memory of it."

"But that's unreasonable!" I exclaimed, "the disgrace is gone."

"Think what the Wade respectability has suffered—no, she will never forgive him. To her he is a criminal still. Personally, I should like to give him a monument to himself."

"What would you put on it?" I asked.

"Alured Wade. Saint and Martyr."

⟞⟞• Banny Firelocks •⟞⟞

The waiter at the Greyhound was a stranger to Luftonbury. He had only been three days in the place. By habit he was a dweller in towns, but he had never yet found himself, for what might be called a temporary permanency, in such a small one. He knew all about Cheltenham and had once been six months in Bournemouth, but the red-bricked, narrow-streeted place, where you might turn a corner to find yourself with one foot on the pavement and the other in the country, was something new. He was a little contemptuous but hardly displeased, being a man of humour and devoid of plebeian loathing for the unexpected. He stood at the window, a rather incongruous figure, light and smart, as befitted a man who had begun life in the ranks of a distinguished line regiment.

Luftonbury sat on the Wye between Symond's Yat and the Severn. The Greyhound, in its Mid-Georgian dignity, looked down upon an open space from which the streets meandered, some towards the bridge, some upstream, some downstream, some towards the hills of Wales.

It was market day, and from the first floor of the Greyhound he watched a spectacle he had never seen before. The space in front of the inn was the recognised repository for conveyances of every sort. The day of motor traffic was not yet, and gigs, taxcarts, drays and wagons, stood wheel to wheel, empty and horseless, their owners distributed about the town. A few saddled horses of inferior lineage and varied callings gave life to the medley, and the ghastly decorum of an ancient pony-phaeton produced a shock in the observer such as a man might feel on meeting his mother in a skittle-alley.

The afternoon was warm and people mopped their faces as they sought their own vehicles, men leading nags and women leading children whilst they struggled with baskets and captive poultry. Harnessing was going on among the sober, the half-sober and even the drunken, and gaps began to show in the wheeled ranks as the drivers pulled out from the throng, settling themselves for the road.

Soon the space got so empty that the waiter had a clear view of the box-like omnibus which plied between Luftonbury and a place some miles west of it. As its neighbours melted away, the singular appearance of this vehicle was thrown up with greater emphasis; and though it stood radiating immobility as a desert stone radiates heat, it was full of women who sat contentedly in it with an aloofness like that of beasts in a menagerie. The waiter could see their silhouetted backs through its windows. His mouth widened as he looked, realising that not one of them knew that a long, lean young man was stretched along the roof above their heads with his ear to the round ventilator-hole that preserved them all from suffocation.

When the driver appeared lugging a pair of horses, he seemed to take no notice of the superfluous passenger, and, climbing to his seat, steering his cumbrous cargo past the Greyhound and out of the town.

The omnibus rolled along. There was a smell of grass and coolness, and soon the distant blue haze of the valley of the Usk began to come up before them.

The bus was officially supposed to hold ten places but in spite of the placards proclaiming this fact, there were eleven people inside. The eleventh was a girl who sat on a bundle in the gangway with her back to the horses and the end furthest from the door, jammed between a pair of elderly women. She was rather blatantly dressed as to colour and had taken off a straw hat trimmed with violet blue daisies and laid it on her knee; by this time her neighbours had learnt every stitch and twist of it by heart. A disapproval seemed to rest on it, shed by their eyes. The girl had a fresh complexion, a large mouth and a head of lustrous, copper-coloured hair. Though her position was enough to show that she was there on sufferance, it was something in the faces of her fellow travellers that brought that truth home. The ten others sat silent, perhaps because the rattling windows and the age of the springs made speech an effort.

At last a woman spoke.

"There 'ere 'at must 'ave cost ye a pretty penny," she observed, lifting her eyes from the daisies to their owner. "Young slips like you warn't used to the like of them rig-ma-jigs in my day."

Banny's lips parted over her teeth and every line of her face seemed to turn upwards. She looked the very incarnation of impudence.

"Twenty-five guineas—no more," said she. "Nothin' to me, of course."

The ten women stiffened. There was a bitter tension; nearly everyone wished to say something memorable but no one could think of it. As the girl knew she could not meet all the eyes turned upon her from different directions, she looked up over the ten heads and met the gaze of a young man who was staring down through the large round gap where the ventilator ought to have been. His face was withdrawn instantly.

She began to laugh, inwardly and soundlessly, and those of her companions who noticed her shaking shoulders supposed that she was laughing at them. The silence grew blacker and blacker. In a short time Banny looked covertly up. The face was there again but a finger was laid on the lips.

"Don't betray me," said the eyes. She nodded almost imperceptibly.

When the others were not looking she glanced up once more. The understanding between herself and the man above was cemented and both smiled. This time Banny could see more of his features and recognised him as someone she had occasionally noticed on a market day, but did not know. She had heard that his name was Mander and that his father did a little horse-coping.

The road lengthened in the wake of the bus, as though the unwieldy thing were a yard-measure, unrolling it as it went. Behind them, a dark speck was growing larger and a high gig with a bay hackney in the shafts was overtaking their sober pace; the ten women had forgotten Banny as they watched it. It contained a farm servant and her mistress, who was driving.

"Matilda Rollitt," announced the passenger nearest to the door, looking round and addressing herself to all. Everyone leaned forward.

The gig was close behind, but instead of passing them, the woman driving pulled back and followed. She was a conspicuous figure, older by a good many years than Banny but younger than any of Banny's companions in all the things that go to make personality. Her eyes sparkled and the hair that escaped from under her hat-brim was curly; though she was too fat and the well-defined curves of her body were disturbed as the bay shortened his pace to her check on the reins, she had a full-blown attraction. Her glance roved to the roof of the trundling ark; its cargo of females seemed to have no existence for her and she called in a bantering voice to someone whose replies came from over their heads. The words were inaudible in the hoof-beats and rattlings.

"Ther' be *a man* up above!" exclaimed a matron in a black jacket. If she had said "a tiger" she would hardly have worn a different expression.

Banny's eyes went to the ventilator but there was no face to be seen, only a round section of a trousered leg.

The talk was tossed from the gig to the roof and back. Sometimes the woman who followed flung up her head and laughed and sometimes a distinguishable word bobbed up throught the noise, like a cork in rapids. Banny could see nothing of her because of the shoulders and straining necks of her companions.

At last the driver pulled out from behind and passed, striking playfully at the roof with her whip. It rattled on it as she disappeared.

"Ah-h—I've seen something of '*er*."

The woman by the door leaned back and looked round, folding her arms, as she spoke.

"Lives nigh you, doan't she, Mrs Pritchard?"

"A bit too nigh, p'raps, if 'er did knaw. Just the archard between me and 'er."

She shut her mouth as if to signify that nothing further would be allowed to escape from it. Her air of finality roused the others. They were not going to let the subject drop to please her arrogance. The black-jacketed woman spoke up.

"Old Rollitt 'ave a blind eye, so ye'd think. She be purty nigh young enough to be 'is darter."

"Not 'er!" exclaimed Mrs Pritchard, stung into opening her lips. "Farty-five if 'er be a day!"

"Thirty-nine."

The voice came from a tiny ancient spinster, so much swallowed up in her shawl that she might have been passed over as a package. Public attention, which had settled on Mrs Pritchard like a butterfly on a bush, now rose and flitted to her.

"Nonsense," said the black jacket.

"I 'eld 'er at the font, I tell yer."

The spinster sat in the silence of achievement. There was nothing more to be said.

"If it isn't one 'tis another," began Mrs Pritchard, determined to regain her position. "I've seen 'er dressed up of a Sunday and smirkin' crewel across the pews to the man as was pullin' the bell-rope in the parch. 'E went red in the face too. Not a smirk out of '*im*. 'E pulled all the 'arder, thinkin' to be done with the job, poor soul, an' away safe with 'is wife in the chancel. But no good, 'twarn't. Them fellers 'as to pull by time, ye see, not by the piece."

Banny listened, open-mouthed. She had only come back from service a few weeks ago. She knew little of the countryside gossip.

"And last market day," continued the other, "she were doin' the 'andsome and 'er eyes rollin' about like marbles. Through a winder I saw 'er sittin', like a duchess in the new eatin'-shop takin' tea with 'er latest, and poor ould Rollitt, as 'ad 'ad a drop too much, walkin' about outside, mazed-like, not knowin' where 'er was. I'd 'alf a mind to step up and 'it smart on the winder an' cry shame on 'er."

"And 'oo was with 'er? Was it the man that rung the bell?"

"Why, 'oo should it be but young Edwin Mander, 'im that she's been carryin' on with this couple o' months? Ye see yerselves, she can't pass a man on the road without makin' a to-do with 'im. Whoever the feller up above is, she couldn't leave 'im alone, strynger or no strynger."

A shade of annoyance ruffled Banny; the rampant femininity in her had given her a certain proprietary interest in the man whose secret she shared and it displeased her to know that he was concerned with another woman. She wished that his leg was not covering the ventilator, that he might hear what some people thought of his taste. She would take care not to glance up at him when she got out. So far, she had rather looked forward to doing so.

She had only had a glimpse of Matilda Rollitt. What business had she to take up with a young fellow like Mander?—she who had a husband and a farm and was not far off forty? She had never happened to see Matilda before, for old Rollitt was a new tenant. Banny's mother was not much over forty and had grey hair; Mrs Rollitt's was not grey, but what did that matter? She could not understand how a young man could be such a fool.

Now that the episode of a gig had banded them together, the women talked on. Banny never raised her eyes from her lap till it was time to put on her garish hat and collect her parcels. As she did so, silence fell on the bus. Her impudence had been forgotten in a newer interest, but now, as they began to pull up, her companions put on an air of oblivious detachment. She edged her way gingerly out and stepped down into the road.

They had stopped before a small, very new-looking public house behind which a path ran over the fields to her home, and among its upstart pretensions the place had a plate-glass window in whose blankness the bus was imaged as in a mirror. Pausing before it to see her own figure, with a view to its possible effect on Mander, she was confronted with his reflection. He watched her with a broad smile. Their looks met.

She turned away haughtily and disappeared round the angle of the Friend in Need.

The women did not notice the window whose dark background of curtains had turned it into a revelation of all they wanted to know. One glance at it would have told them who had been the object of Mrs Rollitt's attention, but they started again unconscious of what they had missed.

Edwin stared out over the hedges at the diminishing form making its way to a solitary cottage and marked the place down in his mind. He had never yet entered the Friend in Need but he resolved to look in before long. He wished he knew Banny's name. Then, remembering the ventilator, he laid his ear as near to it as he dared, hoping to hear something that might give him a clue to the identity of the red-headed girl. He had heard the passage of arms about the hat and chuckled as he thought of it; for his fellow creatures gave him the amusement they often give to a naturally idle man.

"A baggage, for sure," observed the black jacket.

"What can ye expect with 'air like that?"

"Banny Firelocks, they do call 'er, so I were told."

"Just come back from service, I 'eard, in 'ereford. Girls don't get no good in them capital cities. A niece of mine came back from Monmouth, an' no contentin' 'er. Nothin' good enough for 'er to do an' nothin' sarcy enough for 'er to say. 'Don't you think to be'yve like that,' says I, 'or out you go,' says I. 'And let me tell yer, ye'll never get a man as'll put up with yer,' says I, 'not unless ye're a sight better lookin' nor what ye be. Some o' them'll put up with anythin' for a pretty face but you're none o' that sort,' says I. 'You'd scare a dog from a butcher's tray if you was be'ind it,' says I. And would yer believe it, she went out an' put all the clean washin' in the pig's pail, an' off with 'er down the road, 'ome. That's what girls is, nowadays."

Mrs Pritchard stopped for breath. Corroborative and sympathetic noises followed, like applause after a song.

Edwin sat smiling overhead; he was a good deal interested in the girl who had flouted him at the inn door. She had some spirit, that one. She might turn her back but she was not one to give a man away. Banny Firelocks, those old cats had called her. Such a name! He had the usual prejudice of his class against red hair, but somehow he did not mind it on her. The women had got their knives into her and no mistake. He was a trifle out of temper with Mrs Rollitt because he supposed Banny Firelocks had heard her heavy personal chaff and this made him feel rather silly. He lived at the very end of the bus's beat and as its remaining passengers alighted at their respective homes they looked up at him with appraising curiousity sharpened by the events of the journey.

*　　*　　*

Edwin had good opportunities of picking up information, for it was his duty to look after the occupants of the shanty that his father called a stable and there was nearly always a young one to exercise. He had good hands and was not rough with horses and he was constantly to be met about the roads either in the saddle or driving some raw youngster in a gig. It was not long before he pulled up a Roman-nosed three-year-old at the Friend in Need and called to the landlord to bring out a glass of cider. By the time he left he had discovered Banny's name to be Barbara Langland and that her mother owned the cottage across the field and kept fowls. The wench had a tongue, he was told, and was as sharp as a needle with two points. "A bit too many for some of 'em," added the landlord, grinning.

Mander drove on, a little disturbed. He sometimes aspired to be "too many" for other people, himself, and he was not sure how much he liked the quality of too-manyness in a girl. It worked very well with old women in a bus but he felt it might qualify the value of a further acquaintance. He was rather vain and not quite as bold as he made himself out to be.

His vanity had been cosseted by the notice Mrs Rollitt had taken of him; he liked to see people nudge each other in the town when he strolled along with her on a market day. She had not been too many for him and never would be, for her wits were not her strong point. Sometimes he was almost wearied by Matilda's boisterousness and the demands she made on his flattery. As he drove on, thinking of these two women, one of them came towards him round the corner of the lane. The white blouse made her hair the more conspicuous. He slowed down. As they passed each other Banny looked up, hesitated and dropped her eyes. She stopped too, not quite sure how she was going to deal with the situation, though it did not seem to her entirely unpleasant.

"I suppose you won't come for a drive?" he said. The idea jumped into his mind and out of his mouth in one bound.

"Well, you *have* a cheek!" exclaimed she.

"But will you?" persisted he.

She stood considering. Her eyes danced.

He had just put his whip into the socket and he took it out, as though he would go on.

"I might—" said Banny.

He shifted the reins to his right hand and leaned down, holding out the other.

130

"Well, I never!" said she. But she took his hand and stepped up. They drove on, turning into a long lane between the sweet smelling fields.

"This is better than the bus," said Edwin as they went along. "What d'ye think?"

"There's more room."

"And better company, I hope."

She did not answer.

"I like it better, myself."

"Well, you've more business here than you had there," said Banny.

"Oh, come now!"

"What made you get up there?"

"I wanted a lift."

[At this point Edwin Mander evidently put his arm round Banny or made some advance, and in the struggle that ensued her hat fell off on to the road.]

"Now, none o' that," said she.

But Edwin knew all about women. Did he not read the comic papers?

"Don't you pretend you're not pleased, Banny Firelocks."

At the sound of her nickname on his tongue, she turned and slapped him handsomely on the face.

Perhaps it was the sound of the smack, perhaps it was that the astonished Edwin gave an involuntary jerk to the riens, but the Roman-nosed horse plunged into the collar and bolted.

In another minute the near wheel was half way up a stone heap and Banny clung to the rail beside her with all her might. By a miracle they righted themselves and the hedges began to fly by like telegraph poles past a train. Neither said a word, but the sinews stood out on the young man's hands as he sawed at the bit. The horse had a coat like a bear and Edwin knew that a long, steep hill was in front that might help matters if he could only keep the cart straight and meet nothing till they came to it. It was dry weather and the rattling and the hoof-beats almost deafened Banny. She drew her breath in short sobs and her red mane was coming down. When at last the ground rose before them their pace grew slacker, and by the time they had reached the top of the hill Edwin had got the horse in hand. He pulled him up on the summit.

Banny was shaking in every limb. She climbed down and stood by the cart, hatless.

"I'll go back for my hat," said she. "Go you on; I'll walk home."

He made no reply, looking at the blowing horse and the dark marks of sweat under the harness. He was rather out of breath himself, for they had galloped the best part of a mile.

"It was all my fault," said Banny, with white lips. "I'm main sorry."

She turned back down the lane.

Edwin drove on at a walk. Every leaf that rustled in the hedge stirred the three-year-old's raw nerves and he determined to take him home at a steady jog when he had managed to quiet him down. He found it rather difficult to make those soothing noises that horses understand when he was himself so full of wrath. She *was* a baggage. Not a doubt about that. He was very angry and the fact that she had neither screamed nor hampered him in any way did not soften him at all. He told himself that he had done with Banny Firelocks.

*　　*　　*

Banny trudged back in the dust honestly ashamed of what she had done and thinking ruefully that Mander might hand on the tale of her foolish ill-temper and that it might be brought up against her by some jesting neighbour. Her face grew red at the notion. She did not dislike Edwin now, but she would then. She was a long way from home and her limbs still shook from her fright. Her hands were so unsteady that she could hardly twist up her hair and she had lost so many hairpins that it was hard to make it tidy, but she pressed on, for her mother would be looking for her to come back and get the tea.

Mrs Langland's health had been bad of late and because of it, Banny had been obliged to come home to do the rough housework besides attending to the horde of hens that scratched up the path, had dust baths in the garden and sowed the drying green with dirt and feathers. She had found it dismal enough, for mother was exacting and she would have liked far better to return to service though she went about her duties with the thoroughness that was hers.

She was footsore now as she opened the gate, and the fowls, seeing her, ran with ungainly strides from every point of the compass and swarmed about her like street-children escorting a band. She shooed them away crossly. Feeding time was not yet, but she knew she would soon have to turn out again and attend to their wants.

Tea was already spread and she was rather surprised at hearing no comment upon her lateness. She looked across the hearth at her mother's expressionless face: Mrs Langland was taciturn by nature, and the two would sit speechless half an evening. Banny sighed again. She realised that her daily round was a necessary one, but she got wearied at times and tonight she was upset. As though she had read her daughter's thoughts, Mrs Langland spoke.

"I suppose you're a bit tired of this, Banny."

The girl looked up, surprised. It was the most human thing she had ever heard her say.

"And money's getting pretty short with you idle so long."

"I suppose so too," replied the girl, secretly rejoiced. "Then I'd better be looking about for something, d'ye mean, mother?"

"No need for that. I got a place for you today—and you'll need to take it, too."

"Never you fear. I'll take it, right enough."

"It's near home, so you can come in, now and again, to give me a hand."

Banny's face fell. She would have liked to get further afield.

"Mrs Rollitt from Dowling's Farm, out Bowcross way, came here this afternoon. She'd heard you was at home. She's wanting a girl to help her and I said you'd be ready Tuesday."

"But that's too far off for me to be coming over here," said Banny. "It would never do, mother, never!"

"She said she'd give you a lift here every second week. And don't you tell me what'd never do, nor what would. And I tell you I've promised."

"I can't go there. I'd rather go anywhere."

"Yet you was pleased enough a minute ago."

"But I didn't know you meant that. I don't like Mrs Rollitt," burst out Banny

"What's wrong with Mrs Rollitt, I'd like to know?"

"Men," said Banny.

"And what d'you know about it then? An' it's nonsense," she added.

She lived so much apart from her neighbours that all gossip was news to her. He own feelings were her only test for everything and Mrs Rollitt's good natured civility to her that afternoon would have nullified anything she might hear against her. And Banny was her daughter whose opinion could but be negligible.

The girl said no more. Her real objection to taking service in Mrs Rollitt's house was her fear that Edwin might have betrayed her there. At the present moment her sense of having made a fool of herself governed her and she did not realise how unlikely a man of his type would be to tell anything against himself.

But there was no help for it, and the following Tuesday saw her arrival at Dowling's Farm.

She surveyed Matilda out of the corners of her eyes as they stood together in the kitchen and she listened to the list of her duties. No, she did not look forty, thought Banny, to whom forty meant senility; and she seemed so pleasant and easy, with her round pink mouth and sparkling eyes; she was not one to be hard upon anybody. Banny was to help the cook, look after the living room, do the mending, and in the afternoon was to be "dressed" and ready to answer the door, for Mrs Rollitt was in a large enough way of living to have certain pretensions. There was a parlour at Dowling's, with lace curtains that were never drawn back. When the Rollittts ate their meals she was to wait in a white cap and apron.

In the days that followed, she could not help liking her mistress; she was so good natured and there was something in the friendly, empty-headed woman, with her loud laugh and clumsy vanities, that appealed to her strong sense of protection. It would be so easy to injure her or cast her down, so safe to sneer at her, that the fair play in Banny made her resent the derision of Matilda that the cook was always ready to pour into her ears. What really tried her was that Mrs Rollitt would stand talking for an hour, and she was often sorely put to it to get through her work. Conversation with her was an exhausting thing, for an instant's pause in any subject but herself would make her break with cheerful futility into something irrelevant. To try to stem the torrent was like calling out, "Stop!" to a piece of paper blown down a street.

She became daily more confidential. She talked to Banny about her clothes and her friends, about her likes and dislikes, the men who had proposed to her and the men who admired her. The latter subject was a perennial one, and though she had never mentioned Edwin Mander directly, the girl had no difficulty in identifying him as one of the nameless heroes of her discourses. Even with her small knowledge of human nature, Banny could guess that there was not an ounce of harm in her.

*   *   *

[One day Banny saw Mander speaking to someone near Dowling's farm.].

Her feelings of shame were unchanged but her sympathy had gone back to him, impelled by something she had heard whilst she waited at the Rollitts' table.

"Young Mander's not doing any good with that young horse o' his that he was making such a fine job of," the farmer had said. "He was always a baddish shier and he got a fright an' bolted a couple of weeks ago, drivin'. Mander had pretty nigh cured him, they tell me, an' now he can't do nothin' with 'im. A pity too, for his father was expectin' a good price. Rare angry the old man is, A b'lieve. 'Tis bad luck on the lad, for 'e spent a lot o' pains on that there colt, one time an' another."

Banny had been dismayed. She hurried out into the road in time to see Mander walking away.

She set off after him; at least she would have him know how sincerely she regretted the ill turn she had done him; but he turned towards the Greyhound and when he heard her step he looked back.

"Mr Mander—!"

Banny was flushed and her curly lips were parted.

"Please to let me speak to you—I was that glad when I saw you pass by, for I want to say I'm so sorry. Oh, I do blame myself, I do!"

He looked surprised.

"What's wrong?" he asked, pushing his cap back.

"The horse—I spoilt your horse with my goings on that day. It was all my fault!"

"Oh,—that?" said Edwin, airily.

"But I heard your father was angry an' blaming you for it."

"He made a bit of a noise but it didn't disturb me, no fear. And we've sold the horse last week; well, too. It takes a lot more nor that to beat *me*. You're lookin' first class," he added, his eyes on hers.

"I'm that pleased about the horse!" exclaimed Banny, unheeding. In spite of her pleasure, she felt flat. Though no one had suffered for her folly she would have liked him to understand how sensible of it she was, how willing to take the blame.

She put out her hand to say good-bye.

"But you're not going yet," he said, holding it. There was no doubt she was attractive, and the little devil that danced in her eyes was beginning to perk up again.

"I've things to get done" (she was almost going to say "for Mrs Rollitt", but somehow she could not bring out her name to him.) "I must do them before I go back."

"Where to?" said he.

"Home", she said, prevaricating.

"Near the Friend in Need?"

She nodded.

She was going back by train, as she had come, for there was a railway station near Dowling's farm, yet there was a considerable wait to be filled in before it started. They spent most of the time sitting on a bench in the little green public garden near the Greyhound. He had to leave first, and it being early, she sat on; the devil still danced and she had forgotten the flat feeling that her apology had brought about. Her heart was light with relief and with something more. He had made her promise to spend her next free afternoon with him, and though she thought of Matilda Rollitt's dismay should she learn with whom she was going to spend it, she put that part of the matter from her. What right had Matilda to mind? She was married and, above all, she was forty, and she, Banny, was young—young—and the world of men was hers, not Matilda's. It had been a thrilling afternoon.

Her last errand was at the inn. After Edwin had gone, she rose and went up the steps. The waiter, who had watched her from the portico as she neared, came down to meet her.

"You've forgotten me," said he.

Banny stared. There was a faintly familiar look about him, but she was completely puzzled and stood stock still. He smiled and as she noticed the little lines that the smile produced, running outwards from the corners of his eyes, she began to remember. She saw the fallen dusk of a chill May evening lit up with flares, and heard the braying of mechanical music as the arms of the great merry-go-round sprawled against a sky made blacker and bluer and colder by the raw glare beneath it. The air rushed again at her cheeks as she clung far above the indistinct faces of the slow-moving crowd.

"We met in the air," said the waiter. "You may forget, but I don't."

"No, I haven't forgotten."

It was two years since the May fair, that had raged just outside Cheltenham, the one she had enjoyed so much. The fun had grown with the darkness and as the swings flew out wider and wider from their umbrella-like centre of revolution, men, women and children had joined hands or laid hold, each of the nearest flying chair, so that the night was dotted with planetary couples spinning round their particular sun. He had been just before her and had leaned back and held out his hand. After that they had proceeded through space together at intervals for an hour or more and, between their flights, had strolled and talked. Again and again they had gone back to the exhilaration of their pastime and in the end he had walked with her to her door. They parted in ignorance of each other's names, and though he suggested another meeting, she had shaken her head; for she was leaving her place next day and both had accepted their acquaintance as an episode. She thought of the stranger young man now and again but he had finally passed into that shadow of general experience which forms the background of life.

Now, she was only half pleased; embarrassed, astonished; for what she felt most was a pang at finding anything to overlay the pleasure of her afternoon. She would have liked that no figure but that of Edwin Mander should arise to disturb her contemplation of it.

When Banny had gone the waiter retired to his pantry; there were no guests to be attended to at the moment and he sat down beside the sink in his shirt sleeves—for he was careful of his clothes—and gave himself up to his thoughts, which were agreeable ones. Perhaps this was going to be more than an episode, for he had discovered that her anchorage, independently of the chances and changes of service, was only a few miles away. And this time she had told him her name.

Perhaps there was in all Luftonbury no more independent person than himself. He had no parents and the only creature belonging to him was a brother who had melted, somewhat disgracefully, into Australia and of whom he had never since heard. His own want of anchorage never distressed him, and no doubt this detached feeling had made him the more pliable to accept the flash of Banny's hair across his horizon as an episode. He was a contented fellow and very active. Nothing came amiss to him, from football to the study of village crosses, which latter he would walk any distance in his leisure times to examine. Where people were concerned, he was rather critical than social. It had been unlike him to stretch out his hand to Banny in mid air, but he had not regretted doing so; he only regretted that there seemed to be no chance of doing it again. To-night would be his evening off and he was glad, because business would not be easy to attend to in his present humour.

He was now a fixture in Luftonbury and had discovered that he liked the place; his half contempt for it had vanished and he began to find a good many interests; he walked far and wide, and as the Greyhound boasted a veteran waitress who shared his duties, he got an occasional game of football in the field by the river where the young men of the town disported themselves. Country folk were becoming more intelligible to him, both in mind and speech, and as he was nothing if not a student of his fellow creatures, a new range of experiences began to open before him. Now, to crown his interest, he had found Banny and with her reappearance he realised that the detachment of his attitude could not last. She was so definite. . . .

[Soon after meeting Banny again Bob Trent, the waiter, fell into

137

conversation outside the Greyhound Inn with Mrs Pritchard. He had
seen Banny with Mander and took the opportunity to ask Mrs Pritchard
who he was.]

"And what do 'e want to knaw for?"

"He's the dead image of a cousin o' mine," said the waiter, unabashed.

"Then ye'd better ask '*im*. 'E'll knaw 'is own name, I dessay, though
maybe 'e mightn't knaw yours."

"You've got a smart tongue, ma'am," said he. "I guessed you were
pretty smart. That's why I asked you. And I'll be bound you know most
things."

"Well, I don't mind tellin' you," said Mrs Pritchard, realising that she
had found a pearl, "I 'appen to know a good deal about Edwin Mander—
that's 'im. A feller that thinks 'imself somebody."

"And I daresay he's right," said Trent, smoothly, "but 'e's not my
cous—"

"Ho!" broke in Mrs Pritchard, "it might be better for 'im if 'e was.
You're a sensible, civil chap, at any rate. Now that Mander is a good-for-
nothing feller, always 'angin' about women. He's makin' a proper fool of
one I've 'eard tell of that ought to know better. Them that goes with
'orses is always a trickin' lot."

"A horsedealer, is he?"

"They're 'is father's 'orses, not 'is. The old man works 'ard enough.
Edwin goes ridin' about like a lord."

Trent was a good deal perturbed, for that sentence about the woman
who ought to know better sounded to him very ominous. He dreaded to
ask more in case he should find it was Banny she meant and he did not
know how to get at the truth without some revelation of his own state of
mind. To give his companion one glimpse of that would be like putting it
on the placards.

"Not that there ain't excuse for 'im," continued Mrs Pritchard. "She's
always philanderin' about to meet him. I haven't no patience with
women an' girls nowadays. Well, I must be gettin' along. Good day t'ye."

He went into the inn, ruffled. He could not recognise his own conception of Banny in Mrs Pritchard's words, but his heart sank. Had they
not met, he and she, at a public fair and had she not been ready to spend
an evening with him though she had never set eyes on him before? Yet
her high spirits and the pleasure in a man's company that she did not try
to hide were perfectly simple and honest. Even when he escorted her
home through the empty streets she had made none of the advances that

138

many women he had known would have thought nothing of. It had amazed him to find that a girl so full of life and attraction should be able to make it plain that she would neither expect nor tolerate any active demonstration of her effect on a stranger.

*   *   *

Banny's heightened colour and silence about her outing were lost upon Matilda, who was not observant and though the girl's mind ran continually on Edwin's more ardent manner, she went on with her usual energy. As the weeks sped by, most of them bringing an afternoon in his company, her sense of Matilda's unsuspecting ignorance made her the more zealous to please her; she had remorseful moments but she resisted their faint chill. Why should what was fleeting to Matilda destroy what might be real to her?

She went very little to Luftonbury. She came occasionally across Trent and had once walked down to the river with him, and though she felt, even with a certain uneasiness, that he was always there in the background, her thoughts were taken up by Mander. She had not got to the boiling-point of love, though she was coming near to it and until she knew how far his feeling for Matilda really went, she was having sense enough not to let herself be carried away. She had been obliged to tell him at last that she was living under the Rollitts' roof and had been acute enough to see, from his avoidance of her name, that he had not broken with Matilda. Sometimes she would promise herself to be quit of him altogether, yet, knowing herself for a fool, would repent.

*   *   *

November brought the shorter days and it was in the lamplight that she sat sewing in a room off the farm kitchen and heard steps coming to the back door. She took up the lamp and went to open it. As she held it high, to her surprise she saw Trent standing in its shining stream.

"I've walked out to speak to you," said he.

"Will you come in?"

Banny was uncomfortable. She disliked the cook and the prospect of her questions and comments.

"No, thanks," replied he. "Please come out and speak to me."

She did not think of refusing. She stepped out and shut the door behind her. There was a stone bench by the doorway and she set the lamp on it, for it was a windless evening, very dark but still and soft.

139

"I've got to ask you a question," he began.

"Oh, but not here!"

Banny could hear her fellow servant moving inside the kitchen.

"I've disturbed you," said Trent. "I'm sorry, but I had to come."

"They'll see the lamp and be coming out," said Banny. "We'll go a little further away."

For reply he turned out the light. They went to the gate at the end of the flagged path.

"Now, what is it?" said she.

"Is it true you're walkin' out with—anyone?"

She was speechless.

"I've no business to ask, but I'm askin' you all the same."

"No more you haven't—and who with, I'd like to know?"

Her voice shook a little, for she was angry.

"I'm not mentioning names and I'm not wantin' to", said he.

"Then I shan't tell you," said Banny, her temper growing.

He heard her breathing quickly, though it was too dark for him to see her breast heave. Perhaps she was going to cry. He was no bully and his heart smote him; he was also very astute and he had felt, even from the very beginning, that he understood her so well.

"All right," he said. "I'll go. I've had my tramp for nothing."

She heard his hand on the latch of the gate.

"Stop—"

"It can't be helped. I'll be off."

"But what right have you to come here asking me questions?" she cried, her quick feelings, stirred by his defeat, contending with her high spirit.

"None," said Trent, "and I might 'ave known it. It serves me right."

It was no cat-with-a-mouse impulse that made her seek to delay him, for she was incapable of that. What she desired was to ease his mortification; but she meant to save her own face too.

"Tell me who you meant and I'll answer you," she said.

"I meant Mander. I've seen you and 'im walking together more than once."

Neither spoke for a moment and he stood waiting; but he was satisfied, knowing as well as if he had made her that she would keep her word.

"I'm not engaged to no one," said she.

"Well, goodbye then. I'm main glad I came."

"But there's not many girls would stand being asked such things," said Banny, whose independence, in spite of her compunction, was ruffled.

140

"It's true. I should ask pardon for that."

"Oh, no offence," said she, tossing her head.

"And you won't pretend not to see me, nor look the other way?"

"I might and I mightn't."

Had the lamp not been put out, he would have seen the little devil that Mander had seen dancing in her eyes.

"Look here!" he cried, seizing her hand, "It's got to come out! I love you, an' there it is. I've never seen a girl like you—I know it—I've known it ever since the fair. I'm not the chap to take your fancy, I daresay, but I can't 'elp that. You'll never find one that'll love you more than I do. Be quiet and don't pull your hand away like that. I won't touch you. I won't 'urt you. But you must listen now. I never thought to see you again but I've never thought of anyone else since. That's all."

He dropped her hand.

She was bewildered by his vehemence, inclined to be angry, a little awed; uncomfortably aware of some force too large to fit into her experience. Her light high-handedness had joined forces with the little devil and they had fled together like children running to shelter from a thunderstorm.

Before she had time to recover he had taken her hand again. She jerked it away.

"You don't love me, I know," said he. "That's not odd. But do you hate me? Tell me that. If you do, it should be easy to say. Say it, if it's true!"

"Don't, don't! They'll hear us in the house!"

"Say it!" he cried. "Say it, if you mean it!"

"Yes—no! I don't know! leave me alone! There's someone coming!"

The back door opened and a figure stood thrown out by the light. Banny ran past it and up to her room in the attic.

She could hardly sleep that night for perplexity and irritation. She was disturbed by Trent's coming and annoyed with the cook for having worried her. The two girls had almost quarrelled at supper and she had flung off to bed as soon as it was cleared away. She knew that Trent meant what he said and she did not know how much of what he said Edwin meant. How many older women had told her that men were more trouble than they were worth! She supposed that it would be wiser to take no account of men in a general way but she knew that she would not do it. She awoke with a headache and was glad that Matilda had gone off to Lufonbury early, leaving nobody to bother her with talk. The cook was sulking and it was only when Matilda came home later that the welcome quiet of the day was at an end. She drove up, her face blowsy from the sharp air.

141

Banny went out to carry in her parcels. As they entered the house together Matilda beckoned her upstairs.

"What do you think of this?" she said, before she had pulled off her coat. "I hear there's to be great doings at Christmas; a ball at Luftonbury in the Greyhound! The town people are having it and the farmers, and the tickets will be out an' selling a week from now. What d'you think of *that*? And I'm going to get a new dress. I can't make up my mind what style I'll have. I'm going to get it made at Miss Baker's in Queen Street; I think coral pink, don't you? It's so uncommon. As soon as I heard the news I went straight to her shop, and I said, 'You must take my measures.' 'Indeed I will and with pleasure,' she said. 'Coral for you, Mrs Rollitt. You'll be queening it in coral.' That's the words she said. I'm to go next week and try it on and you must come with me to help. It'll be a treat for you, Banny. They're to get a band from Monmouth."

"It'll be grand, I'm sure."

"Yes, but don't you think coral? Or would mauve be better? But then, my hair's dark. Banny, him that I was telling you about—the tall one—he's sure to be there."

"I suppose there'll be a lot of company."

"There's the big room at the back. The dresses will show off well. Coral, I do think."

"I've never been inside the Greyhound," said Banny, her thoughts going to Trent.

The new dress enwrapped the house like a mist; Rollitt, saved from its coral folds by outdoor work, could evade it, but Banny was almost choked in spite of the interest she could not help taking, even vicariously, in gaiety and pretty clothes. All the instincts of her youth and sex told her that she would love dearly to be going to the Greyhound too, notwithstanding the embarrassment of meeting Trent and the possible stab of seeing Mander reft from her by Matilda.

*   *   *

Matilda and Banny entered Miss Baker's door together the following week; the momentous choice had been made and the coral pink dress awaited the first trying on.

Miss Baker was the chief draper in the town and her shop was a darkish place. It was empty but for Mrs Pritchard, who was sitting at the left hand counter waiting for someone to serve her. At the back of the shop a few steps led to the millinery department, from which the tones of its owner could be heard in conversation with a customer. Matilda and her companion went to the right hand counter.

As Miss Baker came down to see her customer to the door, she called her assistant and, waving her towards Mrs Pritchard, turned, with all the suavity that attends millinery, to Matilda.

"The dressmaker will be ready in a minute, Mrs Rollitt; please to sit down. Is there anything else I can do for you?"

"I come 'ere to see Miss Baker," said Mrs Pritchard, loudly, from the other end of the shop, "and ye might let 'er knaw it."

"She's engaged 'm," replied the assistant, a pigtailed girl of fifteen, in an appalled whisper.

"Do as you're bid, child, an' tell 'er I'm waitin'. I've been in this place a good ten minutes. Time's nothin' to some people but it ain't that way with me."

Mrs Pritchard sat near the door while the others were further in. The assistant approached the group and touched her employer's elbow.

"Please 'm," she began.

"I am engaged," said Miss Baker, with majesty.

"I come 'ere to see Miss Baker," reiterated Mrs Pritchard, *very much* more loudly and without turning her head.

Matilda giggled.

"An' I don't go till I see 'er too."

"Excuse me one moment, Mrs Rollitt."

Miss Baker went down the shop and stood by Mrs Pritchard.

"I am engaged with these ladies. Is it anything important?" she enquired.

"I'll thank ye for a penny reel of white cotton and I'd like ye to knaw that I'm not to be put off with a chit of a child with 'er 'air down 'er back."

Miss Baker turned away, purple in the face, and approached Matilda and Banny.

"Come this way, please. We'll wait upstairs in the millinery."

They followed her.

There was no fitting-room, but a screen was drawn across one end of "the Millinery", behind which Matilda and the dressmaker disappeared. Banny sat at one end of it, where she could see the process of fitting. This had hardly begun when Miss Baker, hovering round with suggestions, was disturbed by hearing the footstep of Mrs Pritchard drawing near and seeing her ascend the steps with the apprehensive face of the pigtailed girl behind her. There was no flight for Miss Baker, for "the Millinery" was a *cul de sac*. There was one vacant chair and on this Mrs Pritchard seated herself.

143

"Bring me some trimmed 'ats," she said.

The angels were not on the side of Miss Baker. As, with compelling eyes on her assistant, she pointed to the drawer in which her main stock of hats lay, the sharp sting of the shop-door bell pierced its way to them. The girl dropped the drawer-handle and ran.

Miss Baker approached the drawer, took out a few hats, and gazing over her client's head, displayed them, one by one, with martyred impersonality.

"There's naught to suit me there", said Mrs Pritchard; "I want somethin' a decent woman can be seen in without settin' up for a scarecrow. No blue daisies for me!" she added, looking towards Banny.

Meantime Matilda had got into her coral framework and was turning round and round before the glass, patting herself here and there.

"Is it lively-looking enough, d'you think?" she asked Banny.

"A piece of silver braid across the bodice would do that," said the dressmaker, through her pins. "And I thought of splitting it up the skirt and letting in a sliver braided panel with a touch of swansdown."

"I could wear a silver rose in my hair with it," observed Matilda.

"It would be a nice finish," said the dressmaker.

"I've got one here that's the very thing for you," exclaimed Miss Baker, laying down the hats and diving into a box of trimmings. "Try it, Mrs Rollitt; it's just *made* for you!"

Stretching an arm, she passed the flower round the screen.

At this Mrs Pritchard could contain herself no longer.

"'And me that one over there, please!" she called out, pointing to a black hat on a stand. "I've not got the time to sit waitin' all day to be attended to!"

Miss Baker turned back, trembling with annoyance, and took it down.

Whipping off the one on her head, Mrs Pritchard snatched it from her, put it on and made for a mirror that hung close to where Banny sat.

As she met her own image she started; in her haste she had set it on askew and its bunch of feathers dangled insanely over her face. She looked like some outlandish tropical bird. The reflection also showed her Matilda, bare-armed in the scanty foundation of her fiery coral pink, watching her and stuffing her handkerchief into her mouth in a paroxysm of laughter.

"Yes, you may laugh!" cried Mrs Pritchard. "Standin' there 'alf naked an' burstin' out o' your clothes. Go you 'ome, Banny Firelocks, you're an impudent monkey, as I do knaw, but yer mother should be ashamed to let ye be trailin' about with a man-'untin' 'ussy like that! Good day to 'e,

Miss Baker. There's nothin' you've got that'll suit me, and small matter, too, for it's the last time I cross this doorstep, I promise ye."

She collected her things and was gone.

"To be 'issed through the town—that's what would do 'er good!" she cried, as she disappeared.

Her steps echoed along the bare boards and the metallic stab of the shop bell was like a full stop as the door shut behind her.

Miss Baker was dumb. Such a breach of decorum had never happened in her establishment. Banny was laughing wholeheartedly, her hand at her side, but Matilda's giggles as she was helped into her clothes were becoming rather unsteady and spasmodic.

"She's got no business to miscall me that way!" she said in a vacillating voice as she came out from behind the screen.

Banny stopped laughing for she could see the tears in her eyes, wide and round, like a child's.

"I'm upset," said Matilda, sitting down suddenly.

"Never you mind her—nasty old figure-o'-fun," exclaimed Banny.

"Yes, but I've never been spoke to like that before—not never—it's a cruel shame!"

"Don't take on. She's gone."

Banny patted her shoulder.

"But such names! Did you hear, Banny? I'm sure I don't know what I've done to be spoke to like that. I don't know what anyone would think to hear her. I've never been used like this."

She began to weep stormily. She was one of those amazing women who cry above their breath.

Miss Baker stood by, dismayed; there had been the most disagreeable scene, and now they were threatened with hysterics.

"A cup of tea, Mrs Rollitt. There's nothing like a cup of tea. It will do you good. I'll get it from upstairs in half a minute," she said, disappearing.

By the time she came back Banny had managed to restore quiet. Matilda gulped her tea and Miss Baker returned once more to her own interrupted interests. Banny, whom she had hardly taken account of, now struck her as a good-looking young woman she could not remember having seen before.

"Can I do nothing for you?" she asked. "You are perhaps needing something for the ball too."

"Oh, no, I'm not going."

Matilda looking up from her tea.

145

"I don't know why you shouldn't," she said. "What's to hinder it?"

"But I couldn't. I've no dress."

She was not sure whether she wished to go or not.

"I'll stand you the ticket," said Matilda, "and I'm sure I can find something you can wear, at home."

Miss Baker was a good saleswoman.

"A nice muslin blouse—"

The thing was produced, as though by conjuring. She shook it out before them.

"But I really can't; I can't afford to," said Banny.

"Never you mind. I'll see to that," said Matilda, among whose faults a lack of generosity had no place.

They left the shop with the parcel. It is a hard thing for a girl to refuse a pretty piece of finery, and though Banny felt that she was now committed to what one half of her desired and the other half feared, a little warm thrill of excitement ran through her.

As the day of the ball drew near, she began to have misgivings, and to feel that she risked a good deal in going. What would Edwin do? What would Trent do? He would not be free to flurry her, being far too busy, but how if Mander were to neglect her for Matilda, or how if he neglected Matilda for her? In the latter case there might be scenes she trembled to imagine, though she could not forbear to smile, thinking of his dilemma. It was a faint smile, for she might come back having seen her castle in the air crumble. Not yet had she admitted to herself that she loved Edwin, but the present jeopardy made her believe that she did. She wished that she was not going and could put off the evil hour, if evil it must be. But her acceptance of Matilda's gift had made it impossible to draw back and she knew her mistress would never let her do so, because her good nature was leavened by the desire to show off her conquests to her maid. Banny's weakness had got her into a tight place and her heart ached too. There would be little zest in life if she were to lose Edwin.

The dress had been sent home and Banny and the cook were in the kitchen one afternoon when Matilda came in dressed in it. As she displayed herself old Rollitt appeared in the doorway. His wife's back was towards him, but, as she turned this way and that, they came face to face.

"Well?" she exclaimed, awaiting admiration.

His expression startled the girl. Without a word he went away and out of the house. Matilda broke into an affected shriek of laughter.

146

The farmer crossed the yard, fumbling in his pocket; passing an empty cow-shed he turned in and took out a letter. It was crumpled and soiled, for it had lain in his working coat two days, but he had read it many times, and now, in this deserted place, he read it again.

Mr Rollitt,
> The day will come when you may thank me for writing these few lines. Beleeve me I am a wel wicher. You should have eyes in the back of your head to be up to some women that ought to respek your name, but not she, and my advice is youll see whatll open them at the Greyhound come Friday.
>> A welwicher.
> You may be blind but others sees enough and has done.

The vision of Rollitt's face had made Banny uncomfortable and on the morning of the ball she was thankful to hear him announce that he was not going to it. He had been stonily preoccupied for several days and from the way he watched his wife she made sure that something was wrong; he was an even-tempered man to live with and she had never seen him put out unless the farm work went amiss, nor had she ever heard him say anything sharper than that you might as well hunt grass-hoppers as try to follow Matilda's talk. Banny wondered whether gossip had come to his ears, but now that he was going to stay at home she was easier. His intention surprised her, because, though he had reached the age when most men prefer the placidity of the hearth, he liked company.

*   *   *

Banny was rather in awe of the assemblage they found at the Greyhound that night. A lot of country people were there, young and old, and a piano with a strident cornet was toiling away, for they arrived after the entertainment was begun. She had never been at so great a gathering before. Matilda sailed in, her eyes searching the crowd, and when Edwin, among it, was freed from his partner by the last chord of the waltz and saw the two together, his face betrayed his astonishment. He stopped in a corner to consider what he should do. Banny observed this, smiling with a rather wan amusement; then, as she recognised some girls she knew, she joined them.

Matilda edged her way towards the young man. Another dance began and the two twirled off together. There was no sign of Bob Trent, who was busy in the room where refreshments were set out. Then Banny's companions melted away with new partners and left her to the contemplation of the couple with which she was concerned.

Matilda's face was beaming. Her coral pink dominated the quieter apparel of the other women, for she was one of the few in evening dress. Banny had put on her best white summer skirt and the muslin blouse became her well. She did not know many people, but as several young men were not long in discovering her she was soon dancing. She forgot about Edwin and began to enjoy herself.

The ball had gone on for some time before Mander approached. He had been very conscious of her, and at last it was borne in upon him that if he did not make some effort he might be left out in the cold. But it had not been easy to get away from Matilda and she was watching him sulkily.

Banny's eyes sparkled; she was not one of those red-headed women whose skin, when they flush, reflects their hair. Her dark, positive red locks did not look as if they had boiled over into her forehead, but her cheek was brilliant and her neck, uncovered by the opening of her blouse, as pale as cream.

"You seem to be enjoying yourself," began Edwin.

"You're right there," said she.

She was enjoying his resentful tone.

"I couldn't get to you before."

They were standing by an open door at which, for a moment, Trent appeared. Banny had never seen him in his black clothes and he wore them well and looked smart, for he had a good figure. She nodded to him with a smile, which she hoped that Edwin saw.

Trent's face lighted and the shaft went home to Edwin.

"Who's that chap?" he asked, when the waiter had gone.

"A friend of mine."

"I don't think much of him."

"Well, I do. That's the difference," said Banny, surprised by her own words and wondering if they were true.

They began to dance. Banny had been going up in Mander's estimation for the last hour. In the crowd of women her bright personality shone out like a torch; some were, he thought, too pale, some—especially one—too fat; many were awkward and though Matilda was resplendent, her robust possessiveness was growing irksome; above all, other men's glances put Banny in a new light. The knowledge that he was expected to dance many more dances with Matilda lay heavy on him. Trent was standing at the door again and he knew that his eyes, too, followed

Banny. Edwin promised himself that, once this evening was over, he would take a new line. He had learned his lesson; for the present he would play his part lest Matilda's resentment should fall upon him before he was far enough from her to escape it. There should be no visible cooling on his side tonight; as soon as he was out of her reach he would free himself, once and for all, and it need not matter to him what she said or did, then. After one more dance with Banny he went meekly over to where Mrs Rollitt stood.

The girl looked after him, almost sure that she was not going to lose him. He had only just stopped short of telling her so, and she was so straight a creature that there was no doubt in her mind that any love he would offer would be honest, in spite of his flirtation; and she never doubted Matilda, believing that her spectacular doings were born of vanity and nothing more. And now, in the excitement of music and rhythm and the realisation of her own power to please, the world seemed transformed to Banny and life, for all its household work and small disappointments and much-predicted troubles, a triumphant thing. Her heart was high and Edwin, because the best side of a man has a tendency to rise up, however feebly, when first attracted by a woman of finer nature than himself, seemed to be revealed as hers only.

Yet he had gone off again to Matilda. The glow, through which her excited nerves pictured everything, faded a little. It was so very hard that Matilda, out of pure frivolity, should stand in her path.

It was when supper was over and dancing about to begin afresh that Banny looked up and saw Rollitt at the top of the stairs. A knot of other farmers was round him, and though they were talking, he was taking no notice and looking this way and that. She could hardly believe her eyes, for he had said so much before she and Matilda started, about getting an early sleep after a hard day, and going to bed as soon as they were gone. She had remarked it because his volubility was in contrast to the silent surliness of the last day or two. Now, she remembered he had told the man who drove them to come back to the farm and return to Luftonbury to fetch them later. His wife had expostulated, saying that it was four miles to the town, and he had answered that the horse was coughing and that he'd no notion of his standing in a cold courtyard half the night. He looked flushed but she did not think he had been drinking, for he was firm on his feet and his eyes were purposeful.

She looked round for Matilda, whom she had not seen for some little time. She stood back sheltering herself behind whomsoever she could, terrified lest Rollitt should see her and ask her where his wife was.

149

Gradually, as she began to put two and two together, she saw that he had come to find out what Matilda was doing; he must have heard some talk and now he meant to put its truth to the test. His order to their driver, his talk about going to bed, his grim taciturnity—it all fitted.

Her concern for Matilda awoke afresh as she saw him. She was sure that she and Edwin were together somewhere out of the way, and she was afraid. And standing there not knowing how to act, it occurred to her that what might come of the collision she foresaw between husband and wife, would be the clearing of the way to her own happiness. Even now, she believed herself to be really first with Mander, and that, parted from Matilda, he would assuredly turn to her. Rollitt had gone into the supper room on his quest. Soon he would come out, baffled and furious. She had only to let matters take their course.

She stood with a beating heart and, putting her hand over it she felt the soft fabric of her mistress's gift caress her fingers. How many little kindnesses she had received from the silly woman; how near the easy tears and easy smiles were to the surface of that fullblown, yet strangely childlike, face. The kindnesses moved Banny, but what moved her most was the protectiveness that dwelt in her own soul. She could not bear to think of Matilda in trouble; she could not bear to think of herself doing nothing whilst Rollitt with his lowering face was hunting about for the unsuspecting creature.

He had come out of the supper room and was staring about. His eyes were hard and the flush had left him white.

As he went again to the staircase, his back turned to her, she ran across the floor, dodging the dancers who were begining to fill it anew, and into the supper room. Plates and glass were being cleared away and Trent was directing a boy who was carrying away a basket of knives.

"Mr Trent, Mr Trent!" she cried.

All this evening the waiter, his hands full, had had time for nothing but an occasional peep at the dancers, but he had looked, later, to snatch a few minutes to himself. They were not short-handed at the Greyhound to-night, for extra help had been hired, and he hoped that his chance might come after supper; Banny's greeting had heartened him, and he was determined to see her for a little, if possible. It seemed as if she had not really resented his unwarranted appearance at Dowling's and that was a hopeful sign he had not ventured to expect.

He turned eagerly towards her.

"Mr Trent—please come! Can you tell me where Mrs Rollitt is?" said

Banny, dropping her voice. "I want to see her and I can't find her anywhere. Is there any other room where the company sit?"

Trent knew very well where Matilda was. Before supper the waitress who was his colleague had drawn him to a window looking out on a tiny court. She was a weatherbeaten old girl, waspish but merry, and as she pointed down to it she closed one eye. Mander and Matilda were picking their way round the little place to a door in the shadow. "That's the old harness room," said the waitress. "'T ain't used now, *except on ball nights.*"

"I think I can find her," said Trent to Banny.

"But I must see her myself. *I must.*"

She followed him on to the landing.

Rollitt was mounting the stairs up to the higher regions. He was evidently going to search the upper floor; he was looking intently before him and did not turn his head.

"This way," said Trent, swerving off down a long passage.

He had seen Rollitt too and did not need to be told what was in the girl's mind. At the end of it they came to the back stairs. They ran down. They were dark and she could not imagine where he was taking her, but she kept close behind him. At the foot they stepped out into the sharpness of the night air. Still she followed him till they reached the harness room door and heard Matilda's voice within.

"Miss Langland wants you!" called Trent into the darkness as he opened it. Matilda was standing horror-struck as the flickering light of the courtyard lantern came through the doorway.

"Mr Rollitt's here", said Banny, from behind Trent.

There was sound of someone moving in the back of the harness room.

"Come," said Banny.

Like a child Matilda obeyed her.

The three turned back across the court, Trent leading. Neither of the women noticed that he locked the door behind him as they entered the inn. He turned to Banny, who was shivering from the night air and her own nerves.

"Don't you worry," said he. "Just go up the back stairs to the second floor and turn along to the left. That'll take you to the front staircase. You get your wraps from the dressing room up there, where you took them off, and come down in 'em. I'll see to the rest."

Matilda clung to Banny.

"Don't let him go," she was saying. "I'm frightened."

The girl dragged her upwards. She was too much perturbed to grasp

151

Trent's intentions but she trusted him blindly. As they mounted she heard his feet run along the passage above.

They hurried up to the second floor; the gas in the ladies' room was low, for the wearied attendant had gone to watch the revels. She turned it up and seized the thick garments they had arrived in. She could see that Matilda was much flustered as she hustled her into her coat and out to the staircase.

They looked over the rail. Rollitt was standing below with Trent.

"Yes," Trent was saying, "I saw them go up. They knew you were come for them and they went to get their cloaks."

"But I went up myself. There wasn't nobody there."

"P'raps you don't know the new ladies' room, sir—how should you?" said Trent "You've to go through a swing door—there they are, coming down!"

One effect that the sight of the two cloaked women had on Rollitt was to determine him not to go out again into the December night till he had warmed himself, inside and out. He was not altogether satisfied, but he could find no peg on which to hang his suspicions and the bar into which he was towed by a brother farmer was mighty pleasant after his drive in the open cart. His wife knew that when he got into company he liked he would stay there, and soon she recovered from her adventure and was ready to dance again. She was relieved to find that Edwin was nowhere to be seen for she did not want to have anything more to do with him whilst Rollitt was about. She prepared to finish the night cheerfully.

Banny was tired; she would willingly have gone home and tried to forget herself and the puzzlements of life in sleep. She wondered at Matilda's inconsequence and at the small impression things appeared to make on her, and she suspected, now that she and Trent had pulled her out of her scrape, that she would go on very much as before. The thought of Mander lurking in the back of the harness room was not to Banny's taste; she would have called it farcical, had she known the word, but she only knew that the remembrance of it was disagreeable. The dancers were getting fewer and she refused to dance because her feet ached from the unaccustomed thinness of her soles.

The supper room was empty. Such men as were not dancing were in the bar, and Trent, having spent more time than he intended away from the thousand and one things he had to deal with, had gone downstairs. There were a few chairs in the room and Banny sat down and closed her eyes. The joyless vigil of those who must endure to the end of a festivity at which they no longer care to be festive was on her. Half an hour went by.

She was aware of someone coming in and opened her eyes to find Mander beside her. She could see that he was very angry.

"A nice thing that damned waiter did to me!" he exclaimed—"turned the key of the door when he let you in, the fool, and there I've been rattling at it and banging the window and not a soul to hear till a boy looked out and let me in. I've been in that court ever since."

"It's a good thing for you the waiter was anywhere about," said she.

"What was it to him where I was?"

"Nothing," said Banny, "and it was me made him go after you. I wasn't going to have Mrs Rollitt get blamed for being out there with you."

"Jealous, that's what it was. And you sent him out to spoil sport."

It seemed to Banny that there was something mean in his face; something she had seen there before yet had not allowed herself to acknowledge. She forced the thought down anew.

"Go away," she said. "I'm tired."

"I tell you I'll be even with that sneaking waiter! If I thought the feller knew what he was doing when he turned that key I'd make him sorry he'd ever seen me. I can't abide the sight of 'im."

"Well, who cares? Not him, I fancy."

"I'll get him sacked, see if I don't."

"You'd better stop that," she said, her face hardening. "I'm not in the humour to be bothered. Leave me alone, can't you?"

"You're a vixen an' no mistake. If you don't take care I'll go an' not come back. That wouldn't please you. And yet you're glad, I believe, that I was locked out."

"You're always laughing about other people, but when a funny thing happens to yourself you don't look at it like that."

"I'm off. You'll be sorry for your temper some day."

She was lying back in her chair. For answer she turned her head away.

He looked down at her for a minute and then went to the door. Here he stopped. She did not move.

"Now Banny," he said, turning back, "don't go on like this. I know what's up with you right enough, and don't you make any mistake."

"Are you going?"

"Not me. I've more sense. I tell you I don't care a curse for that fat old woman that's been making a fool of herself over me this year past. I don't care what becomes of her—it's not my fault that she's always running after me—I'm sick to death of her. Have no fear about that!"

Banny sat up fiercely.

153

He went on, her angry eyes spurring his ill humour. He spared Matilda nothing.

"Stop that!" she cried, hotly. "I won't hear another word."

He paid no heed. The indignity of his position, shut out in the courtyard, the evening tied to one woman when he wanted to be with another, and now Banny's repulse, loosened his tongue. Matilda's folly, her age, her vanity, the foolish things she had said to him; he poured them all out. He read nothing in the girl's disgust but a passing offence because of the time he had spent with Matilda Rollitt. He was outraged because of its inconvenience. She was carrying it too far.

She sprang up and made for the door.

He caught her by the arm. She tried to fling him off but he held her.

"Take your hand off me or I'll call out!"

He saw that she meant it and loosed his hold. She ran out and, halfway across the ballroom, met Rollitt.

"Come on," said the farmer. "We're going and Matilda's waiting."

The three went downstairs together. Their cart was in the yard of the inn, among others, and they went out to it, husband and wife first. Banny followed, hampered by the getting on of her wraps.

Trent was outside and came up to her.

"Good night. I mustn't keep them," said Banny.

"But shall I never see you again?"

"I must be quick," said she.

"But will it be never? You can't mean that?"

"Oh, no! Sometime."

He dropped back, thankful for that much, and watched them drive out of the lighted yard.

As they passed under the arch she looked back and waved her hand.

"Cheer up," he said to himself.

*   *   *

Christmas passed and New Year; it was a cold winter and spring came slowly. Matilda had never taken the risk of letting Mander come to the farm and now, for various reasons, he did not attempt to seek Banny there. It seemed impossible to run across her anywhere; though he had written to her twice he had received no answer. He had even gone so far as to waylay Mrs Pritchard, who lived near enough to Dowling's to be able to tell him something about its inmates; but as she supposed him to be wanting to hear of Matilda, she gave him no news and any profit got out of their interview was got by her.

It was near the end of April when he heard that Banny had left her place and was at home with her mother, and on the first Saturday after this discovery, he went down to the Friend in Need. He had resolved to make another attempt to go back to old relations and he thought, if he hung about on the chance of her coming across the field, he might wait in the inn and step out as she passed by. There was no other way from the cottage to the road and she would not be able to avoid him. Saturday was a likely day for her to be going out. He remembered that the further window of the bar looked straight towards Mrs Langland's cottage. This suited him well and he ordered his beer and sat down on a bench from which he could conveniently see out. There was no one in the bar but himself and the landlady behind the counter.

At last he saw the cottage door open and the girl come out. Her mother stood talking to her on the threshold; perhaps she had sent her on an errand. But as Banny neared, Mander saw that she was dressed in her best and gathered that she was going out for the afternoon. He thought he would not approach her in sight of the inn windows so he drew back till he heard her come past and turn into the road.

He watched her from the shadow of the porch.

She was going quickly and when she passed a stile that was by the wayside, a man vaulted over it.

It was Trent. He put his arm round her and kissed her.

They walked on together.